MURDER IN PROVENCE

BOOK 3 OF THE MAGGIE NEWBERRY
MYSTERIES

SUSAN KIERNAN-LEWIS

SAN MARCO P

D1410131

Books by Susan Kiernan-Lewis

The Maggie Newberry Mysteries
Murder in the South of France
Murder à la Carte
Murder in Provence
Murder in Paris
Murder in Aix
Murder in Nice
Murder in the Latin Quarter
Murder in the Abbey
Murder in the Bistro
Murder in Cannes
Murder in Grenoble
Murder in the Vineyard
Murder in Arles
Murder in Marseille
Murder in St-Rémy
Murder à la Mode
Murder in Avignon
Murder in the Lavender
A Provençal Christmas: A Short Story
A Thanksgiving in Provence
Laurent's Kitchen

An American in Paris Mysteries
Déjà Dead
Death by Cliché
Dying to be French
Ménage à Murder
Killing it in Paris

Ella Out of Time
Swept Away
Carried Away
Stolen Away

PROLOGUE

The failing evening light wove through the gaps in the wicker-backed chairs like golden strands of hemp. There was a faint fragrance of garlic and lemon in the air as the many lower street bistros prepared to satisfy their patrons with special renditions of *paella, cassoulet* and *soupe de poisson*.

The warm caressing light and delicious scents should have made Catherine's walk more enjoyable as she negotiated the rough cobblestone road to the stretch of unembellished, middle-class apartment buildings where her aunt lived.

She held her breath to hear the soft tinkle of wine glasses and dinner plates being set down on starched tablecloths or the sounds of laughing and talking on the breeze that scooted inland from the sea.

Yet she heard nothing. The bistros and outdoor cafés were out of sight and silent from this distance. One would think all of Cannes was deserted.

Why hadn't she gone the longer way round? Past the bustling restaurants and the slapping water of the moored sloops in the tiny harbor? Why did she always have to take the short cut, look for the quick fix? She'd worked late at the hospital again tonight.

How stupid! Or was it greed? Were the three hours of extra pay worth the risk of being late to her aunt's special dinner? She had reasoned that by taking the back streets to her aunt's neighborhood she would lose nothing. Nor would she have to pay the exorbitant charges a taxi would demand to take her there from the bus stop. No, this was definitely the smart thing to do.

The dormant, dark windows on either side of the close alleyway stared blindly down at her. The cobblestones themselves were damp and gritty even though there had been no rain recently that Catherine knew of. Then the alley—too small to allow even the smallest of compact cars—narrowed even further.

She approached the last turn before the final climb up ancient stone steps to the row of tidy, bland apartments where her aunt lived. She quickened her pace and looked back over her shoulder.

There was nothing behind her except the alleyway with its movie-set back prop of shadowy buildings and the darkness that seemed to swallow up her trail like a treacherous mountain shelf that slowly crumbles into oblivion as each footstep leaves it.

Catherine hurried to stay ahead of it.

She held her breath again and listened a second time for any noise other than the sound of her own heart beat pounding in her ears. At what point had she become nervous? she wondered with surprise. When had she stopped thinking of work and which doctor had said what and when, instead, had she become aware of how dark it was getting and how lonely this street was?

This time when Catherine held her breath to listen, she heard it.

Her hand tightened on the bag over her shoulder. The two bottles of *vin de pays* in the bag were heavy.

A muffled lumbering sound of something moving unnaturally across the cobblestones, reverberated softly in her brain.

Catherine began to run.

1

The heat was blistering. It poured into the open window of the dining room like a malevolent odor, creeping into the fissures and cracks of the plastered walls and wooden floors until there was no room in the farmhouse not stifled by its invasion.

Maggie stood in the door between the dining room and the kitchen trying to avoid the swelter of the kitchen. She watched as her husband Laurent scooped up the chunks of white fish from the *bourride* and placed them in a baking dish in the oven.

Laurent was six foot five, and his size and activity seemed to fill the farmhouse kitchen as he moved from stove to oven, picking up utensils from the counter and cracking eggs in a china bowl as he moved.

The kitchen was the only room in the house that had not yet been remodeled. Its ceiling arced to an apex that held a large circular skylight and its cabinets were glass-fronted to show the colorful, mismatched bowls and plates within.

Maggie poised her pen over the notepad in her hand. She was a small woman with long dark hair to her shoulders. This morning she had it pinned up off her neck, which accented her high cheekbones. Her eyes were brown and fringed with thick lashes. She watched Laurent as he worked.

"Why not just leave the fish in the soup?" she asked. "Seems like a lot of trouble to put it in the oven when you're just going to return it to the soup later."

Laurent gave his developing *aioli* another push of the food processor's button. He didn't look at his wife. His light brown hair hung to his shoulders and his eyes were dark, nearly pupilless. Maggie always found them sexy but a little disconcerting too, because she could never read them.

Those eyes were a lot like Laurent, himself, she'd discovered. He was a big, handsome Frenchman ...with a mysterious past.

Maggie waited impatiently for the loud whirl of the machine to stop. She knew he was being difficult, but she would wait him out.

Laurent seemed to be examining the top of the stove where a large copper-bottomed cauldron of boiling potatoes sat. Finally, he turned off the food processor and stuck his finger into the golden yellow goo.

"Laurent, I want to know..."

"It's just the way it is done," Laurent said, not looking at her.

"Well, great, I guess that would be a new approach for a cookbook. I'll just write: *'Take the fish out of the soup for no good reason that I can tell you and keep it warm until you're ready to return it to the soup.'* That sounds good, Laurent, and I'm sure housewives all over America will accept these little French peculiarities as special to the region."

Laurent didn't answer as he grated a rind of orange peel into his simmering fish broth.

"You said you'd help me with the cookbook," Maggie said. "Now, if you don't *want* to help me..."

She snapped her notebook shut and crossed her arms in front of her chest.

"*Chérie*," Laurent said with a heavy sigh, "I agree you must find something to do but this..." He waved a hand between the two of them, the frustration pinging off him.

Maggie instantly felt contrite. Did he look a little tired these days? Was *she* the reason for that?

"Sorry if I'm being a pest," she said, raising up on tip-toes and kissing him on the lips.

"*Il n'y a pas de quoi,*" he murmured, rubbing his hand up her bare arm. "It is too hot in here. Why don't you go out into the garden? I will join you when I am finished."

She nodded and he released her, turning back to his stove. Maggie picked up her notebook and a tumbler of sweet tea from a coaster in the living room.

Her little poodle-terrier Petit-Four looked up sleepily from the couch but gave no indication of wanting to follow her outside. She crossed through the living room and left the house through a pair of French doors.

Domaine St-Buvard was a stone farmhouse connected to forty acres of prime vineyard that Laurent cultivated for the light *vin du pays* he produced called *Vin du Domaine St-Buvard*. He inherited the house and the land from his uncle two years earlier when he and Maggie decided to move to Provence for a trial year to work the land and live in the house. Before the end of that year they decided to marry and to stay in France.

Although not an unhappy decision for Maggie, it was still not one she was totally comfortable with either. Her language skills had improved a bit in her two years deep in the heart of Provence, although she still insisted that she and Laurent speak English at home.

The farmhouse had never once been a ruin as all the large older homes in Provence seemed to have been at one time. It had withstood its share of upgrading over the years, especially in the plumbing and bathrooms, and had never been allowed to sit vacant and unloved.

As was common throughout Provence, it was built with fieldstones from the rough surrounding landscape. The roof was made of terracotta tiles and bright blue shutters dotted the otherwise austere façade. Like most self-respecting French domiciles, the house had a garden.

In her first year in Provence, Maggie had been content to simply enjoy what was there, watering when necessary. The garden had been choked with wild geraniums, roses and lavender. Several gnarled olive trees led from the cracked and ruined terrace to the grape fields, and a hedge of wild cherry trees and *canne de Provence* wound around the four stone columns that punctuated the small garden.

After that year, Maggie planted pansies and azaleas in the garden to remind her of Atlanta. A small gardenia bush—sent with much trouble through French customs by her mother—stood wilting in the harsh *Provençal* sun. It hadn't bloomed all summer and Maggie fully expected the first breath of the harsh *mistral* to turn its glossy green leaves into so much tattered confetti swirling across the French countryside.

Laurent had rolled his eyes when she'd planted it, suggesting that she try to grow yellow Canary Bird roses instead or even encourage the wild periwinkles that grew so effortlessly everywhere else around the farmhouse.

Now, as she looked out over the sunbaked garden, her iced tea dripping condensation down her wrist, all she could see were the hardy, bright geraniums and Laurent's extensive herb garden.

She sat in a wooden folding chair next to the large terrace lunch table. It had lately been too hot to eat outside even under the shade of a large sycamore that stood guard outside the French doors. The table was covered with twigs and leaves. Maggie brushed off a clear space and opened her notebook.

She had started this cookbook project in order to have something to do. She hated the sound of that. It made her feel useless and spoiled, like her image of a country club housewife trying to decide which tennis outfit to wear. But the truth was she was unemployable in France as an advertising copywriter —her job back in the States—and she'd never developed a hobby.

Friends back home in Atlanta cooed their envy with comments like: "Oooh, what I wouldn't do with a whole year in the south of France! No kids, no job, a husband who does all the cooking! You're living the life!"

Maggie stared out at the lush green vineyard attached to the property.

Laurent's obsession, she thought, and then caught herself. She knew it was only because she was idle herself that she resented his work.

She flipped through her notebook. It had been Laurent's idea that she work on a *Provençal* cookbook. Perhaps with some kind of theme that set it apart from all the legions of other *Provençal* cookbooks. She felt a sudden wave of annoyance.

This is ridiculous! Me, writing a French cookbook? What I know about cooking you can read on the back of any frozen dinner microwave package.

But in the end, she'd agreed to try because it seemed more interesting than studying French verbs, trying to coax an American familiarity from the dusty garden, or writing wistful letters home to Atlanta.

Laurent slipped onto the terrace from the house.

"Ah, you are thinking, yes?"

"Not about the cookbook, I'm afraid," she said. "I got sidetracked into reflecting about my life."

"Lunch is ready, *chérie*. I must leave by one."

Maggie frowned and looked at her watch. "You're leaving right after lunch?"

"I must see Jean-Luc about fixing the stone wall on the southern—"

"I don't believe this." Maggie tossed her notebook across the table. "We were supposed to work on the book together. You said we would—"

"*Enough*, Maggie!"

She could feel the frustration bristling off of him.

"I cannot write this book with you," he said, his eyes snapping. "I have told you this before. It is not for me to have one more..." he groped for the word, "...task," he finished with exasperation.

"I don't suppose this *meeting* of yours will involve drinking *pastis* and laughing it up at *Le Canard* in town for a couple of hours?"

"We are meeting at *Le Canard*, yes. We will drink together, yes."

"*Naturellement*," she said, not looking at him.

He swept an arm in the direction of the vineyard. "I must tend to my own work."

"Fine, do that." She hopped up and grabbed her iced tea glass. "Lunch ready you say? How nice." She turned and walked back into the house.

Laurent swore softly to himself and, after a moment, followed her inside.

"No, no, can't you see? The sky is hot! It's hot, hot! Where did all this blue come from? Is blue *hot*?"

The small woman turned abruptly away from the hunched shoulders of the sour-eyed young man and faced the classroom of adults.

"Is blue hot?" she repeated.

Her students dutifully shook their heads. One or two murmured a soft, "*Non, Madame.*"

Marie Pernon smiled at the young man and placed her

hands on her hips. Her dark hair, laced with gray, was pinned in a graceful twist at the back of her head. Her eyes were deep brown flecked with gold.

"I'm sorry, Madame," the young man said, pushing away from his table easel. "I want to make it a hot day but I keep making it look cool."

Madame Pernon clucked her tongue in admonishment. "Blue is a very good color, Robert," she said, pointing to the smeared washes across his watercolor paper.

"But you must make it a *hot* blue, yes? How do you do this?" She turned to face her classroom, each student perched in front of a small wooden table or floor easel, their canvas papers clipped in place. "Can anyone tell us how to do this?"

A blonde woman, sitting in the middle of the class, raised a tentative paintbrush in the air. Her intelligent face was smooth and pale against her fall of golden hair. The fingers that held the brush were stained the color of lilacs.

"*Oui*, Madame Van Sant?" said Madame Pernon with a smile. "Can you help us?"

Grace Van Sant cleared her throat.

"My French isn't too good," she apologized. "But if Robert were to...I mean...what about if he mixed more warm colors *with* the blue? I mean, would that just make mud?"

"Excellent, Madame Van Sant!" the little teacher cheered. "*Formidable! Oui,* Robert." She reached over and expertly dabbed up a brushful of aureolin mixed with ochre and then brushed the edges of the young man's azure sky.

"I am adding warmth, yes? I am adding heat to the day, do you see?"

The class murmured that they did see. The young man watched his watercolor and nodded.

"Of course, you must do it when the first wash is still wet, you understand? To blend the colors. Now, add more blue to your sky, Robert, and make it a deeper blue, okay?"

"More blue?"

"Yes, of course," Marie said. "And why do I say that?"

"Because there are reds in a darker blue?"

"Of course, *chéri*. And what is red?"

Robert reclaimed his brush and began to gingerly pulse at his painting with its tip.

"It's hot," he said, visibly pleased with himself for the first time all morning.

"*Bon.*" Marie grinned at the class. "And now, what do we know today?" She strode to the large eastern windows that stretched the length of the studio and took her place on the raised platform at the front of the room.

On the platform were an easel and a table where bottles of faintly colored water stood beside a wooden palette splashed with vibrant watercolors.

Although it was August and hot in Provence, Marie was dressed in all black. She wore dark stockings under a narrow black skirt and a clinging long sleeve jersey. She settled on the stool in front of her easel and leaned her elbows against the table.

"It is true," she said, "that sometimes the color we want is as it comes out of the tube. And that's good news for us in a world that is not always easy. But nature comes in many colors. Infinite colors, you see? More than a paint manufacturer can dream of to put into a tube. And so the color of the light which comes from the sun—which is red and orange and yellow and yes, blue and violet and green—must be blended together to reflect this light as it bounces off things. Robert's sailboat in the *Gulf of Napoule*, for example, Natalie's bowl of aubergines, and Madame Mercier's boy in the lavender field—all must feel this light and show it in a way that only we as the artists can present it."

"What about in the middle of a rain storm?" Grace Van Sant asked. The rest of the class laughed.

"*Non, non,*" Marie scolded them. "It is a good question. There is light, of course, in a rainstorm—even a rain full of black and gray. There must always be light. And next time, we will address exactly that. For now, my dears, please, continue your painting. We have less than a quarter of an hour left to work today." She winked at Grace.

Grace Van Sant. Lovely, talented and smart. So much like Marie's own Brigitte. Marie's friendship with the beautiful and wealthy American was a surprise in many ways. It was not unusual for a rich foreigner to spend a summer or even a year in Arles to play at painting.

After all, where else? Arles is the Mecca of all true artists, even before Paris. Was not Arles the home to Van Gogh? Did not the light produce more wonders here than any place on earth?

So, of course, she knew many foreigners. They were not rare in this part of Provence. But her friendship with Grace *was* rare. She found herself smiling at the thought that she could be so charmed by an American.

Marie began to cap her paints and rinse her brushes and her thoughts turned in anticipation to tonight's dinner. Brigitte and Pijou would be there. They didn't come home as much as they used to, she mused sadly as she squeezed wet color from a small sponge. They had lives of their own, of course.

As the busy wife of a successful doctor, Brigitte had her hands full with charities and making a home for herself and Yves.

Pijou, the single girl with her own life of excitement, flitted off to Paris, Madrid or Rome whenever she had a break from her job. Marie often remarked to her husband René that it was amazing how very different the two girls were. Especially for twins.

As she looked over her students at work, Marie thought

how René would be cooking most of the afternoon to prepare for the girls' arrival. She smiled at the image of her husband rushing about to the local *boulangerie* and *boucherie* to make everything exactly right.

Everything must be perfect for Brigitte and Pijou. From the exquisite garlic mayonnaise to the *legumes farcis* that René would lovingly stuff and baste in testimony to his complete adoration of his two beautiful daughters.

Marie watched Grace as the American applied a broad wash of color to her paper. *Such confidence*, Marie thought as she watched the serious expression of her friend at work. *Such certainty and self-assurance.*

As she continued to watch Grace—her brow knitted in concentration and effort, her large brush dabbing emphatically at her paper—Marie's thoughts strayed once more to her daughter Brigitte and the lightness in Marie's heart faded.

2

"The first year is always the worst. During my first year, I thought Windsor was trying to kill me. You know, like in *Gaslight* with Charles Boyer and Ingrid Bergman? He was such a pig."

"I can't imagine Win being a pig. He's so sweet." Maggie reached for a pitcher of cream across the little café table and squinted at Grace in the glare of the afternoon sunlight.

"Maybe it was the sight of a woman crying every night that made him pig-like."

"You cried every night?"

"For practically the full first year."

"Why?"

Grace shrugged and rearranged the assortment of napkins stuck under the chin of the bored eight-month-old baby on her lap. She looked at Maggie and grinned.

"Isn't she precious? She spits up like this at home too. I don't know why I cried so much. I guess because I thought marriage was going to be like my parents' marriage."

"Your parents have a good marriage?" Maggie frowned. It

seemed out of character to think of Grace wanting to emulate stodgy old rich Republicans. She nearly said so.

"Well, traditional, anyway. Daddy's very attentive to Mother. Always touching her shoulder, pouring her wine first, scurrying to the door to make sure she doesn't have to come in contact with the doorknob."

"Sounds like a butler."

"Exactly. I never told you? Mother married the butler. Jolly nice fellow and he's so tidy."

"Very funny."

The bright sunlight flickered through the leaves of the sycamore that shaded their table. A gentle breeze produced shifting shadows over the little cake plates and espresso cups. Grace's baby Zouzou sat in Grace's lap and reached for the dishes with chubby fists.

This sort of day in Avignon of shopping and café-sitting was something Maggie and Grace had indulged in frequently before Grace's youngest was born. Since then, the excursions to Avignon or Aix had been fewer and fewer.

Although Grace was certainly rich enough to have attendants and nannies—in fact, had one for each of her two daughters—she was very hands on with the children, especially the new arrival who was a buoyant, pleasant contrast to her difficult seven-year old sister, Taylor.

Taylor was a musical prodigy, gifted at the piano as well as the violin. She was also a trial to her parents and a hard child to like. Zouzou, on the other hand, was a baby to adore.

"She never fusses," Grace had said to Maggie with amazement. "Even when she's being pinched by Taylor, or hungry and wet, she just shines through."

Grace and her husband Windsor had met Maggie and Laurent two years earlier. Grace and Maggie, both American expatriates, had begun a friendship. Although Grace's French was better than Maggie's and she was too rich to share many of the same problems that Maggie had, the two had quickly bonded nonetheless.

"This cookbook idea isn't even my idea," Maggie said, bringing the *demitasse* cup to her lips. "It's just Laurent's way of getting me off his back. I don't know anything about cooking and he's completely unhelpful about letting me watch him cook. He's always saying I'm in the way and getting on his nerves. A great first year for newlyweds, you know?"

"But you're a writer, Maggie. I thought the whole point was that you didn't have to know anything about cooking to write about it. Why not interview chefs in the outlying villages? Maybe they'll have wonderful anecdotes to throw into the mix."

"My heart's not into it," Maggie said.

"Madame Van Sant! *Bonjour!* How are you?"

Maggie looked up to see three people striding toward their café table. The leader, a small, athletic elderly woman, waved at them as they approached.

She arrived breathless and immediately bent down and exchanged kisses with Grace before scooping up the baby in her arms.

"*Et voici petite Zouzou, n'est-ce pas? Ohhh, elle est belle!*" she cooed before turning to Maggie. "And this must be Madame Dernier, yes?" She jostled Zouzou on her hip and extended a hand to shake Maggie's. "*Enchanté* Always I am hearing about Maggie this and Maggie that. And this is my husband and my own little girl."

She turned to indicate the handsome, older man behind her who was kissing Grace, and a frowning young woman who stood mutely observing the entire scene.

"René, Pijou, *voici Madame Dernier, une bonne amie de* Grace."

"Maggie, darling, you've heard me talk about Marie, my art instructor? Please, join us, Marie. And so this is Pijou? *Je suis très heureuse de faire ta connaissance, Pijou.* Your mother talks of you often."

Pijou said nothing but sat in the proffered chair while her father pulled in two chairs from nearby tables. Marie settled into one of them with the baby on her lap and covered Grace's hand with her own.

"She is exquisite, Grace, your Zouzou. You must let me paint her. Babies are wonderful to paint, especially happy babies."

"What are you doing in Avignon?" Maggie asked.

Marie made an expression of mock horror.

"You have not been to the show?" She looked at Grace and shook her head gravely, wagging a finger at her. "I thought this was the reason we are seeing you in Avignon. *'There is Grace,'* I said to René, *'She has come to the abstract impressionist show just as I have advised my entire class.'*"

Grace laughed. "I'm sorry, Marie. The lure of the sale was just too much. But I found a lovely bargain or two."

As if Grace needs to hunt for bargains, Maggie thought with a smile as she finished off her espresso.

The waiter came, seemingly annoyed that there would be more work for him and he might have to, presumably, suffer through a larger tip, coldly took their orders and left.

Maggie studied the new arrivals while Grace and Marie chatted in French. It was obvious that Marie had once been a great beauty. But she was an expressive woman and years of lively animation had worn grooves in her face that blander women would not have.

As a result, her face, even relaxed, had a look of perpetual tension. Her dark, graying hair was long and wound tidily into a loose bun that nestled against her neck, with just a few tendrils escaping to frame her heart-shaped face. Marie looked like she was over sixty but she was as charismatic and alluring as a movie star.

Marie's husband René, who looked closer to seventy, was big and handsome. Maggie imagined Laurent might look like him at that age. René was robust and full of good humor, as if a smile were always tugging at the tips of his long, gray mustache. She wondered if Laurent would ever sit in the company of a group of women and smile adoringly at her while she talked with a friend.

And then there was Pijou, who was too old to be a sullen teenager but was broadcasting just enough ennui at the whole social gathering to be considered at least mildly rude. She was slim and tall in contrast to her stout father and diminutive mother. She was also fair and had a pleasant face, if not quite pretty. She dressed almost in opposition to her mother's artistic, dark, flowing clothes by wearing a tailored jacket and slacks. Her ears were covered with rings and studs. Her tastes may be different from her mother's, Maggie thought, but it was clear she'd inherited a sense of style.

Maggie caught Pijou's eye and was favored with a brief smile, followed by a rolling of her eyes as if to seduce Maggie into joining her in her boredom.

"And so you will talk with Jacques, *n'est-ce pas?*" Marie turned to Maggie.

"Jacques?" Maggie asked, looking from Marie to Grace and back again.

"Jacques would be good," René said, nodding. "He would be very good."

"Of course, you must also talk with René," Grace said taking the baby back from Marie who seemed to relinquish her reluctantly. "René is a marvelous cook. He made a meal for Win and me that was incredible. When was that, Marie? A month ago? I'm still stuffed from it. I made such a *cochon* of myself!"

The idea of beautiful and elegant Grace Van Sant making a pig of herself was too absurd an image to form in Maggie's brain.

"Jacques is a chef?" Maggie asked Marie.

"*Oui!* A wonderful chef, and Grace is right. You must, of course, interview René. He is as good as any chef in France!"

René chuckled, shook his head modestly and beamed at his wife.

"So there you are, darling," Grace said airily. "Two chefs to interview—both of them friendly and not about to rip your tonsils out if you ask a dumb question—not that you would—and so to hell with Laurent." She turned to Marie. "Who, by the way, is a wonderful cook too and very hunky besides."

Marie touched Maggie's sleeve.

"The creative process is so important, Madame Dernier," she said. "I understand it very well. Sometimes the blank paper, the empty canvas...I know, it is as terrifying as facing nude all your enemies at once, eh? I know."

Maggie felt a rush of affection toward Marie. "It's been really hard to get started," she admitted.

"*Bien sûr,*" Marie said. "But to write a cookbook! In France is there anything so noble?" She patted her flat stomach, "Or as satisfying?" Everyone laughed. Tiny Marie hardly looked like a hearty gastronomic.

"I have *une idée merveilleuse,*" Marie said. "You must come to my studio tomorrow. Grace, *ma chère,* you will come too, yes? In order to make your friend more at ease?"

Marie turned to Maggie without waiting for a response from Grace.

"You will see my studio and the work I am doing, and René will make you an exceptional lunch, okay? Is that good?"

Marie turned to Grace and put her thumb under baby Zouzou's chin. "And so it is settled, yes?"

Grace laughed a silver bell of a laugh and looked at Maggie who found herself laughing too.

∾

The sky was Naples yellow. Marie used patches of newspaper to blot out areas of color, then filled in the gaps with streaks of indigo and cadmium red while the sky was still wet. It gave the painting the appearance of softness she was looking for.

She stood in front of the oversized paper clipped to a board that measured three feet by six feet and nodded. It was a good start. And perhaps not this painting or even the next two that she would begin just like it, but before the end of the week, she would have the effect she was looking for. She touched a tree into the damp paper with a flat brush.

The phone rang. She paused, hoping René would answer it but soon tossed down her brush and strode to answer it herself.

"*Oui?*" she said crisply, an artist interrupted at her work.

"*Maman?*"

Marie's irritation vanished and she began wiping paint from her fingers onto her smock.

"Brigitte! What a nice surprise! Is everything all right?"

"I'm sorry, *Maman*, you were working, weren't you? I hoped Papa would pick up."

"*Ça ne fait rien, mon chou!* I was finished for the day anyway. Everything is all right?" she repeated.

"Of course," Brigitte replied. "I just wanted to call and see how you were doing. With all the business about the murder, I knew you'd be worried."

"Yes, of course we were worried. Someone at Yves' hospital? Did you know her?"

"A little. She was a nurse who worked with Yves sometimes." Brigitte cleared her throat. "It was such a terrible business. Look, *Maman*, I'm sorry I couldn't make it for dinner the other night. Was Papa too disappointed?"

"Not too bad," Marie lied again. "Is Yves feeling better?"

"Yes, he's better." The quiet unhappiness seemed to slither out of the receiver.

For a moment, Marie was speechless. Then she said, "Brigitte, you must come home. Can you come tonight?"

"Don't be silly. I *am* home. I'm sorry about the other night but I'm really busy at the—"

"I would like to talk with you, *chérie*. I need to see my daughter face-to-face and talk."

"Well, *Maman*, no one would like that better than I would..."

There was a strain in Brigitte's voice and Marie had the sudden, horrified thought that she was in the process of receiving a "duty" call from her daughter.

"...but I've got a husband to take care of and my responsibilities as volunteer charity director at the hospital and I can't just drop everything and drive to Arles. You understand, Marie?"

Marie hated it when her sophisticated and too-grown-up daughters called her by her first name. It usually indicated a condescension that heralded an attempt to hide something from her. She found herself growing upset.

"*Chérie*, I think you need to come home."

"My home is with Yves here in Nîmes."

Marie's eye strayed to the watercolor she was painting. From a distance of eight feet, it looked much more right. Random patches of dry, stark white paper jumped out of the gray landscape giving believable bursts of light. Marie was surprised at how successful the painting was—and that she hadn't realized it.

"Of course," she murmured. "I just wish...your father and I are sorry not to see more of you."

"You see Pijou quite a lot? She says she's always dropping by."

"I suppose she is," Marie said, her eye tracing the soft and hard edges of her work.

"Well, there you are, and we'll get together soon, I promise."

"Yves is all right?" Marie asked.

"I told you he was. He's fine."

"Treating you well, is he?"

"What's that supposed to mean? He treats me like a princess. He treats me *too* well."

"Don't be ridiculous."

"Well, don't insinuate things. '*Does he treat me well?*' You know what you're really asking."

Marie looked away from the painting and felt her shoulders sag within her artist's smock.

"It's for this very reason I don't come home half as much as I could. You're always trying to paint Yves as if he were a wife-beater or something. For crying out loud, Mother, he's a doctor! And a beloved one! Everyone adores him at the hospital."

Marie was alarmed at the tearful tremor she could hear in her daughter's voice. Brigitte was not one given to crying.

"*Mon chou,*" Marie said, frustrated with the restrictions of the telephone.

"Just forget it," Brigitte said, her composure nailed securely back into place. "But just know one thing, okay?"

Marie braced herself for the pain.

"Even if he beat me every night, *I love him.*" Brigitte's voice was shrill. "Do you understand? *He's the one I want.*"

"Oh, Brigitte," Marie whispered through her own tears.

"So, I'll talk to you soon, Marie. Give my love to Papa."

Marie stood holding the phone. Slowly, she set it down and then looked back at the painting. There wouldn't be the interim attempts after all, she thought.

This time, she'd gotten it right the first time. She moved toward the easel, hugging herself as she walked.

Sometimes we can look too closely, she thought, *and see it all wrong.*

René popped his head through the studio door. "Was that the phone, *chérie?* I was cleaning the oven."

"It was Brigitte," Marie said.

"Yes? Everything is all right?"

. . .

Grace Van Sant smoothed out the creases in the red Prada scarf that draped from her shoulders. She decided her merino wool jacket and pleated skirt looked impeccable whether she was crushed into a sitting position behind the wheel of car or striding down Cours Mirabeau.

But then, that's quality, she thought with satisfaction, as she pointed her jet-black Mercedes in the direction of Maggie and Laurent's large *mas*.

She loved their little village of St.-Buvard. Perched on the side of a hill with the remains of a Roman aqueduct at its base, St-Buvard was tinier than most French villages around the area of Aix-en-Provence, Avignon and Marseilles.

With only one *charcuturie*, one newsstand, and one café, St-Buvard was indeed small. That was precisely why she and her husband Windsor had decided to settle near here over six years ago.

They lived in a small renovated chateau ten kilometers outside the village and although it was true Grace spent more time in Aix than in St-Buvard, she claimed ownership of the provincial little town as if she'd been born there.

Grace pushed in a selection of music from her dashboard CD player and the sounds of Puccini's *O Mio Babbino Caro* filled the car.

She drove quickly through the village, nodding at the ancient post mistress who scowled back at her, past the tiny Catholic church on the outskirts of town, and finally over the stone bridge that separated the road from hectare after verdant hectare of planted vineyard.

She drove alongside a low stone wall, rolling down her driver-side window to catch the fragrance of lavender and sun-drenched grass and trees.

It was a spectacular day. Warm and bright and clear. The

colors of the landscape, usually so mild in Provence, seemed to jump off the horizon. She wondered if it was her new interest in painting that made her more aware of the colors.

The deep blue of the grapes mingled with a delicate pallor of lilac, and the sky wasn't just blue as she'd always thought but blue and aqua and pink and green.

Grace tried to imagine how she might capture the sky on paper, remembering that Marie said a proper watercolor artist ought to try to paint at least one sky a day.

Ochre, definitely, she thought, *over a wash of the barest blue.* Beyond that, she wasn't sure. The music welled up inside the car and she touched a button to roll down all the windows to share the sound and so that the countryside scents might engulf her.

Maggie was waiting for her at the end of her gravel drive-way. She wore black leggings and a tailored gray *tablier* that she must have picked up in the village. A blue silk scarf was knotted at her throat.

Grace knew that Maggie cared little to nothing about what she wore, but she still had her own distinct look. Grace thought Maggie's outfit suited her quirky, winsome friend beautifully.

Maggie opened the passenger side door and slid in.

"God, Grace, you look like you drove through a wind tunnel."

Grace laughed and touched her wind-tossed hair.

"I guess I got a little carried away with the beautiful day. Isn't it scrumptious? How are you? Is Laurent home?"

Grace backed the car up and turned around in the drive way.

"He's getting ready to perform surgery on a few wayward vines. He and Jean-Luc."

"How is Jean-Luc? I don't think I've seen him since all the trouble last year."

"He's fine," Maggie said. "He and Danielle are together now, you know."

"I think that's great. Don't you?"

"I think she could do better. Jean-Luc's old."

"Maggie!" Grace laughed and glanced at her friend. "They're contemporaries, darling. He's no older than she is."

"He seems it."

"Do they live together yet?"

"Are you kidding?"

"I guess that means no."

"At least not while her husband is still alive."

"Do you hear anything about him? Win and I are so out of touch with local gossip."

Maggie rolled up all the windows in the car.

"Laurent said he heard he'll be getting out sometime this year and rumor has it he'll get an annulment when he does—if you can believe anything so ridiculous—and then I guess he'll do us all a favor and disappear."

Grace frowned and turned the car onto the A20 highway in the direction of Arles.

"Why do you say the annulment is ridiculous? You're in a very strange mood this morning, darling."

"They've been married for nearly twenty years! Doesn't that sound a little ridiculous to you? To get an annulment after twenty years? Why not just get a divorce like the rest of the world?"

Grace turned to look at Maggie who was biting her bottom lip and staring out at the landscape, made bleaker and more colorless by the intrusion of the super highway. She turned the music down.

"Well, you know," Grace said, "Danielle and Eduard never had any children. That helps their case of annulment. And of course, if they were to *divorce*, Danielle, who is a good Catholic, would have trouble if she ever wanted to remarry." Grace watched her words sink in as Maggie's face softened in understanding.

"Eduard knows that Danielle and Jean-Luc want to be together," Maggie said thoughtfully, still staring out the window.

"Prison gives even the hardest of heads sufficient time to work things out."

"I guess that's noble of him," Maggie said.

"What's wrong, Maggie? Do you want to talk about it?"

Maggie shook her head. "It's just me," she said. "I don't know if I'm homesick or bored or not meant to be married or what. Let's not talk about it, though, okay?"

Grace's brow puckered in concern. "Are you sure, darling?"

"Yes." Maggie turned the music up. "I want to concentrate on the day. I've been looking forward to it." She twisted in her seat and looked in the back of the car. "Where'd you stash Zouzou? She with the nanny today?"

"That's right," said Grace, as she accelerated and changed lanes. She had told Marie they would be there in time for lunch. "It'll give us a chance to concentrate on something besides her darling self. Babies can be quite involving. You and Laurent ought to get a few."

"God! That's all I need!"

"Could be exactly what you need."

"Don't start with me, Grace," Maggie said, laughing. "I have to get the married thing sorted out before I can move on to the baby thing."

Thirty minutes later, Grace and Maggie were seated in Marie and René's spacious salon sipping *rosé* and munching roasted sweet peppers and anchovies. Marie's apartment was situated between the busy downtown shopping district and the outdoor food market in Arles.

The cobblestone streets that wound around the storefronts afforded no sidewalk, and automobiles were forbidden from noon to midnight. As a result, mopeds, scooters and bicycles jetted by in a constant stream, but the romantic impression of an old world setting was kept intact by the absence of car fumes and engine sounds.

The Pernon home was built in the Italian tradition with wrought ironwork inside and out. Situated on the *Rue de la République*, its balcony—which hovered majestically over a gigantic, wooden door with a brass loop knocker the size of Maggie's head—looked out over a jewelry store, a small *boulangerie*, and a *tabac*.

The sun poured into the salon from the French doors creating big squares of light on the terracotta floors. The wide entranceway swept into two salons. The first, where Grace and Maggie now sat, was furnished with hanging tapestries, heavy velvet drapes lined with bulbous gold tassels, swirling burgundy wallpaper and an English Regency sofa with two mismatched chairs. There were three oil paintings in the room, landscapes, but nothing of Marie's work. When Maggie pointed this out as Marie ushered them into the room, the tiny painter shook her head.

"I do mostly *aquarelle, n'est-ce pas?*" she said, holding Grace's hand but talking to Maggie. "In this room, the light, wispy colors of the watercolor would be lost, yes? Be assured, Maggie, my paintings are evident in all the bedrooms upstairs." She pointed over her head.

For a moment, Grace was struck by the up-to-now unthinkable thought that Marie was insecure about her work. As quickly as the thought came, she banished it. Just because she did not hang her own work in her front salon did not mean she was not intensely proud of it.

Because the day was warm, the tall, ceiling-to-floor windows were open onto a small back garden. Grace thought she could smell the scent of lemons and rosemary coming from where she sat.

René entered the salon and greeted them. He hurried to Grace and kissed her soundly on both cheeks, then vigorously shook Maggie's hand, welcoming them to his home before retreating back into the steaming kitchen.

Grace thought Marie looked tired this afternoon. She had never seen the woman with anything less than boundless energy and enthusiasm. She patted the damask seat next to her own and motioned for Marie to sit down.

"Honestly, Marie, René's doing all the work, you lucky woman. Come sit down, or you'll make me want to jump up and start polishing something."

"But you have come to see the studio, yes?" Marie said. "Come. Bring your wine. It's just in here." She led them through the ten-foot double doors of the second salon.

Larger than the family's living room salon, Marie's studio was awash with golden *Provençal* light, its floor-length windows unencumbered by drapes or curtains of any kind. The floor was bare and polished to a shiny gloss. One corner of the room was draped in a thin canvas and it was here that Marie's easel for her work in progress was set up.

The light in this corner was intense. Grace, who had seen the studio one time before, could imagine that every nuance of the paper texture would show up as vividly as moon craters under the sharpness of the light here.

Several of Marie's unfinished pieces, in varying sizes, were tacked or taped or clipped to boards on the walls around the room or propped up on the floor.

Grace saw a flamboyant basket of fruit that Marie had been working on a few weeks ago and was reminded once more of the woman's brilliant manipulation of turning color into the essence of light. The painting wasn't completed.

A series of streetscapes lined one wall, each more startling and colorful than the one before. Grace had asked to be allowed to buy one or all of the series and had been regrettably refused. Marie was eager to sell what she called her meager little Sunday market pictures to the tourists but resisted parting with her real work.

"These are fabulous!" Maggie exclaimed. "I mean, the light in this one, it looks like the sun is coming through from behind the paper."

"*Exactement*," Marie said, pleased.

"And here, how did you capture this shadow? I mean it's dark but the overall feeling is of light and, I don't know...enlightenment."

Grace turned to Marie and sighed.

"I'll never be this good. Why am I even bothering?" She waved her hand at the paintings. "This sort of thing can't be learned in a class, Marie. How awful of you to make us think we could be artists." She smiled at her teacher.

"Grace! To say such a thing!" said Marie, who was obviously pleased. "You enjoy the process, no? It is fun, is it not? To create? To make a pretty thing from nothing?"

Grace shrugged as if unwilling to give up her *faux* petulance. She was teasing her friend, and praising her, and she finally saw that Marie was beginning to relax for the first time since they had arrived.

On the way home, Maggie asked Grace to drop her off at the little stone footbridge about a half a mile from the end of her driveway at *Domaine St-Buvard*. The hot weather had finally relented in the late afternoon and Maggie wanted to take advantage of the coolness.

Plus, she wasn't ready to be home yet.

As she walked along the roughly paved road, the wide sycamores hovering overhead in a protective huddle, she allowed herself to finish the job that the luncheon wine and the enjoyable afternoon had started. She stretched the muscles in her calves as she took long strides down the road, enjoying the feeling of mild exertion after the lazy lunch.

To her right was Laurent's vineyard. Just eighteen months ago, it had been nothing more than black stubs of rubble, burned nearly to the last vinestock by their neighbor Eduard Marceau, Danielle's now estranged and imprisoned husband.

Maggie had seriously doubted that the vineyard would ever come back. She couldn't have guessed that after the care and love that Laurent had poured into it before the fire, he would have had the heart to replant.

She'd been wrong. Last year's harvest was nearly nonexistent. This year's would be poor.

But next year.

Those three words ran through her mind incessantly: *But next year.*

She turned the corner in the road where the farmhouse was now visible and smiled. It really was impressive, she thought, appraising its cold and proud silhouette, in the fading afternoon sunlight.

As she approached, she saw Jean-Luc's old truck parked in front of the house.

Surely they've finished stitching up vinestocks by now?

She hurried the last hundred yards to the front door, her tension rising as she walked.

"There you are, *chérie!*" Laurent called out as she entered the house. "We wondered if you were staying in Arles for dinner."

Laurent was standing in the living room with a glass of red wine in his hand. Behind him sat Jean-Luc Alexandre and Danielle Marceau. They both smiled at Maggie.

"I walked the last bit of the way," Maggie said, smiling. "Danielle, how have you been?" Maggie leaned over the older woman and exchanged kisses with her. "You look terrific."

She settled down on an overstuffed chair opposite the couple and took the wine glass Laurent handed her.

As her earlier vision of a hot bubble bath slowly receded from the evening schedule, Maggie listened patiently as Danielle shared the latest village news and gossip.

"You could have imagined I'd be tired after my day," she said.

Laurent stood in the kitchen and carefully polished the bottom of a copper saucepot. He did not answer.

"You know Jean-Luc does not rank at the top of my list of people I care to see," she said, his silence further aggravating her annoyance.

"I did not think that list included Danielle."

"Don't twist my words. It's nothing against Danielle and you know it. I was not in the mood for company tonight."

"That was *évidemment*."

Maggie bit back her response and took a deep breath. The clock in the kitchen showed it was nearly midnight. She went to the dining room and stared through the French doors that opened to a smaller outdoor terrace. Unlike the larger patio off the living room, this terrace led nowhere. It was simply a small slate patio that afforded a good view of the vineyards.

Now, as Maggie stood looking out into the night, she could almost imagine the sweet fragrance of Confederate jasmine back in Atlanta. For a moment, tears welled up into her eyes.

Am I really so homesick? Is that the base of my problem with Laurent?

She scanned the blackened horizon but the night had erased the view save for the few scraggly rose bushes that huddled outside the French doors. She leaned over and smelled one of the pink flowers. It was fragrant, but too faint to be mistaken for jasmine.

"They are beautiful, no?"

Laurent came up behind her and placed an arm around her shoulders.

"The roses of Provence are fragile to look at," he said, touching one of the petals. "But tough against the harsh sun and wind." He kissed her. "Like my American Maggie, I think, in many ways."

Her mind felt constantly full of prickles and nettles that constantly undermined any sense of peace or acceptance in this place.

Why was this all so hard? Why isn't Laurent enough? Will there ever come a time?

Maggie turned in his arms and tried to let the sweet night and this moment engulf her emotionally as well as physically.

3

The following Saturday, Maggie sat in the garden of *Domaine St-Buvard* with her laptop, her notes from the week, and an iced coffee. Laurent's *potager* was redolently evident to her left.

Clumps of parsley and English thyme interspersed with radicchio, beets, spinach and radishes were planted at the door leading into the house so to be always ready to be plucked even while one of Laurent's stews simmered or as the grill was getting hot.

Maggie thought the idea of a *potager* terribly handy and debated for a moment about putting a sidebar in her cookbook to describe the benefits of having an easy-at-hand herb and vegetable garden. Deciding it was probably more trouble than the typical American cook was going to bother with, she decided to mention it as a quaint French custom but skip the how-to details of actually creating one.

She took a sip of her iced coffee. Laurent was in the vineyard today. If she squinted she could just see him in the distance, dipping down as he examined a rootstock, pruned an errant branch, or repaired one of the wires that stretched endlessly between the grape vines.

Domaine St-Buvard had belonged for generations to a large French family who had owned most of the property in the area —not just the immediate vineyard now attached to the house.

The wine production was prolific enough and the wine good enough to be bottled under its own label, which eliminated the need for a co-op. In the early 1930s large tracts of the property was divided up and sold off to create smaller private vineyards, and so a co-op was formed to help area vintners get their wine bottled and to market.

Maggie looked at her notes and frowned. As usual, she found it difficult to concentrate on the cookbook. Her outline so far was a sketchy framework of Laurent's favorite meals and a few dishes she had enjoyed at local restaurants and had asked Laurent to duplicate at home.

The hook for the cookbook had originally been *The American Palate in Provence*, but Maggie was finding the phrase increasingly vague.

What is *the American palate*?

Cheeseburgers and Coca-Cola—as Laurent believed? Southern fried chicken and banana pudding?

She stood up and tossed her pencil onto the table. Perhaps she should get rid of the whole idea of the American Palate. Maybe she should just let the book be written by an American and let readers draw their own conclusions as to how qualified she was to write a French cookbook.

Originally, she'd thought writing a cookbook meant transcribing a bunch of recipes from various cooks in the area. She considered adding a line or two to give it some color along the lines of: "*If you can't find the briny Sea Bass of Marseilles at your local Kroger, any good white fish will do.*"

It occurred to her that if the cookbook felt this difficult to write, it might also be basically unpleasant to read. She sat back down and picked up her notes again.

A hummingbird moth hovered on whirring wings in front of a stand of lavender bunched in profusion against the house. The moth's tiny wings were a blur of color and motion among the purple flowers.

She heard the landline ring inside the house and felt another pinch of annoyance.

Her cellphone was virtually useless out here in the country-side with Internet access on her laptop so spotty as to be nonexistent. Laurent didn't care since half the time he didn't even carry his cellphone.

It's like living in the Dark Ages, she thought as she retreated indoors and picked up the receiver.

"Hello?"

"Don't tell me you're not coming. I will not speak to you again if you have the nerve to tell me..."

Maggie laughed. "God, you beg off from *one* measly dinner party *once* in your whole life and it follows you forever."

"Only when it's one of *my* rare dinner parties."

"*Once.* We had to back out *once.*"

"I love that! Not *regretfully declined* but *backed out*. So, what are you wearing and are you ~~presently~~ wearing it?"

Maggie glanced at the clock and realized that she was, in fact, running late. She wasn't dressed and Laurent wasn't even in shouting distance.

"It isn't formal, is it?" she asked, trying to look through the French doors to see if she could spot Laurent.

"Formal? Do you mean floor-length formal? Or just best-jewels formal?"

"Grace, do knock it off, won't you? The kids must be with the nanny for you to have so much time to cut up on the phone."

"I knew it. You're not even dressed."

"Bye-bye, Gracie."

"Okay, okay. We'll see you there. And, Maggie..."

"Yes?"

"It's somewhere between blue jeans and your wedding dress, okay?"

"You're a peach."

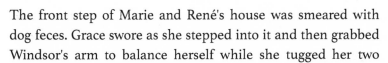

The front step of Marie and René's house was smeared with dog feces. Grace swore as she stepped into it and then grabbed Windsor's arm to balance herself while she tugged her two thousand euro Manolos off.

"Can you believe this?" She looked around the deserted street as if preparing to find the hound responsible. The streets were quiet and dark. All motor traffic was restricted and Grace and Windsor had had to park some distance away.

"Do they have a dog?" Windsor asked.

"I don't know if they have a stupid dog," Grace said, scraping her shoe against the slate stones of the courtyard. Their voices echoed back at them in the empty street.

"Maybe they'll have something inside to scrape—"

"Windsor, don't be ridiculous." Grace pulled her shoe back on and rapped sharply against the door. "Marie would be horrified. I mean, you give a dinner party, you want the table to look nice and the flowers to be just so—and, 'oh, by the way, darling, you've got dog shit on your front steps.' Do not say a *word* to her."

Windsor shrugged and carefully sidestepped the mess.

"There's a lot of it everywhere in Provence," he said. "The French like their dogs."

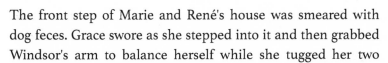

Maggie sipped her wine and felt the firm reassurance of Laurent's thigh pressed against her leg. Marie and René had welcomed them into their home and they sat now with Marie and her daughters Brigitte and Pijou.

And best of all, Maggie had even beaten Grace to the party.

"And so you have an agent back home, yes? To help you get the cookbook published?" Brigitte smiled at Maggie. She was stunningly beautiful. If she and Pijou really were twins, Maggie thought, they were definitely fraternal.

Brigitte's hair was dark and glossy and hung in waves to her shoulders. Her amber eyes seemed to glitter as they moved from Maggie to Laurent.

"Well, no," Maggie said. "The idea is that first you spend all the time and effort in writing the thing—"

"With no guarantee of a publisher at the end of it," Brigitte said, shaking her head. "I admire your tenacity. What keeps you going?"

Laurent coughed and Maggie resisted the urge to spill her drink on his hand.

"Oh, various things, I guess. Faith in myself, I suppose."

Laurent coughed again.

"Darling, why don't you have a cigarette or something?" Maggie asked sweetly. "Perhaps it'll help burn out that nasty cough."

A knock at the door heralded the arrival of Grace and Windsor. Marie rose to admit them.

Brigitte's husband stared out a window, not bothering to mask his boredom. Marie had mentioned by way of introduction that Yves was a physician at the hospital in Nîmes. Maggie took note of how he sat with his arm draped around Brigitte's shoulders.

Like he owned her.

Seated across from Maggie and Laurent were Pijou and her boyfriend Claude. He was a thin, pale young man with wispy black hair, who seemed nervous and was randomly plucking at the multicolored threads in Marie's camelback sofa.

Pijou, who was falling out of her haltertop, was friendlier today—especially to Laurent. Maggie was accustomed to the effect Laurent had on women and, although not totally comfortable with it, was at least not as bothered as she used to be.

The only saving grace to it was the fact that Laurent was rarely aware of his attractiveness to other women. This feature, Maggie thought with a smile, was one of his dominant charms.

"Darlings! You're here! And ahead of us! *Quelle surprise. Quelle* effing shock, in fact," Grace said as she and Windsor were ushered into the salon.

Maggie embraced Grace and then waited while Laurent did the same. It embarrassed her a little that she and Grace—both Americans—would practice the French custom of kissing on the cheek even after the briefest of absences from each other. But Grace wouldn't have it any other way.

"Marie, I love the walk to your home," Grace said happily as she shed a lime green chiffon stole onto the sofa. "So quiet and spooky. I thought I could hear the voices of Roman soldiers echoing across the cobblestones as we walked. Win, maybe we could block traffic to our little *pied-à-terre?*"

Maggie made room for her on the sofa and laughed.

"Grace, you'd have to block off the whole D538!"

General laughter rewarded her and she grinned at her own wit.

Marie stood next to Grace. "Well, with our Grace," she said teasingly, "*Qui sait?*"

More laughter. Maggie noted that Yves looked on with interest now. There was even a smile playing at his lips when Grace entered the room.

Claude continued to worry the sofa's threads. Marie took their drink orders and, promising that dinner would not be much longer, joined René in the kitchen.

Pijou turned to Grace and made a face.

"Guess you heard about the nurse that got killed in Cannes?"

Grace smiled and looked uncertainly at Maggie as if hoping this might be the beginning of a joke.

"Yes?" she said.

"You've heard of it?" Pijou repeated.

"Everyone's heard of it, Pijou," Brigitte said. "And sick to death of discussing it endlessly. The nurse was from Yves's hospital," she said to Grace and Maggie. "All the nurses agreed that Catherine was foolish to take a shortcut after dark. This isn't the fifties, you know. You have to be careful."

Maggie shook her head. "Did you know her?" Her eyes darted to Yves as if inviting him to join in the answer. He ignored her.

"Yes, a little," Brigitte said.

Yves snorted. "You did not."

"I did," Brigitte said, her face blushing.

"*Si tu dis,*" he replied, retreating to his isolationism.

"A sweet girl," Brigitte said to Maggie. "It made me sick to hear of it."

"She was raped and beaten to death," Pijou offered. "Her family couldn't even identify the remains. Yuck."

"How awful," Grace murmured.

"Do they know who did it?" Maggie asked.

"No," Pijou said, "and they probably never will. You don't know our police. It's been two weeks since the killing. The trail is ice cold."

"And so, of course, will the food be if you do not come at once!" Marie stood in the doorway to the salon, holding a wide tray of sparkling drink glasses in her hands.

She smiled at her guests but looked meaningfully at Pijou who shrugged and got to her feet.

"I believe," Marie said brightly as her guests filed past her into the dining room, "that tonight, Brigitte and Pijou's papa has created a true masterpiece!"

The high paneled walls of the dining room were covered with beautiful oil paintings in heavy gilt frames. A waist high mahogany bookcase ran around the entire room filled with books bound with leather covers and stamped in gold.

Along the top of the bookcase Marie had clustered a busy array of memorabilia and art: silver teapots stuffed with quivering, pale peonies; little folded silk fans in soft green and pink; black and white family pictures displayed in antique silver frames. Two large matching lamps with bold pleated paisley shades flooded the dining room table with light.

The guests seated themselves around the painted nineteenth century French country table, which stood in contrast to the traditional tone of the room. Maggie realized that it all worked well together, but she would never have believed it without having seen it.

"You will have to use this meal in your book, *oui*?" Marie said as she set Maggie's soup bowl down in front of her.

René bellowed "Marie!" from the kitchen.

"You are writing a book?" Yves asked Maggie from across the table.

"Of course, she is," Brigitte said. "Haven't you been listening? A French cookbook."

"You are a cook?" Yves asked, speaking to Maggie but looking at Laurent.

Here we go again, Maggie thought. "Well, not as such," she said.

"She cooks," Laurent said.

Maggie nearly dropped her spoon.

"I...." She stared at Laurent in disbelief. "I...do?"

"Can you not cook, Maggie?" Laurent asked, a little loudly. "Do you not know how to cook or are you like some bride from America who cannot make a meal for her husband?"

Maggie wasn't sure where this was going but she had an idea it had nothing to do with her. She looked at Yves who was staring at Laurent.

"Of course, I can cook," she said evenly. "But the book is about the kind of cooking that great chefs do, not mortal housewives. Of course, I can cook." She looked for help from Brigitte or Pijou. "I mean, who can't cook?"

"I can't," Grace said simply.

Oh, great, thank you, Gracie.

"Are you two going to slug it out or what?" Pijou asked, waving her soup spoon between Laurent and Yves.

"Pijou, do not be ridiculous," Brigitte said, her face darkened with anger while her eyes stayed focused on her soup bowl.

"I mean, don't feel bad," Pijou continued. "Yves can't get along with anybody, can you, Yves? My parents loathe him."

"Pijou!" Marie and René came into the dining room carrying two platters of *paella*. "Whatever you are saying, I am sure it is not worth listening to, so kindly, stop."

Marie gave Grace a tired look and then tacked her smile back in place.

Yves slowly turned to René who was standing in the doorway.

"Just a misunderstanding," Yves said soothingly. "Just Pijou being Pijou."

René's face hardened. "May we have one dinner where we do not have some ugliness that must be trotted out to sit among us?!"

Pijou hopped up from her chair and hurried to her father.

She gave him a kiss on the cheek and pulled him to his own place at the head of the table.

"Yves *said* it was nothing," she said. "Just my usual hijinks and you never minded my mischief before, Papa. So, come on and let us enjoy this wonderful meal you've prepared for us. I am starving and ready to eat both platters. And just look at the size of the husband Maggie has brought to your table! Are you sure you've made enough? He's awfully big!"

The table laughed and Laurent grinned good-naturedly.

"So, everybody, sit, sit!" Marie said as she deposited her platter onto the table. "And no more talk of murders," she gave a look to Pijou, who, having salvaged the mood, returned to her chair with a buoyant air.

"Or taxes or news that the Arles Amphitheater is crumbling or anything else that will detract from a good evening with family and friends," René said.

"And new friends too." Marie picked up her wine glass and raised it in the direction of Laurent and Maggie. "We are glad you are among us. You make us better, stronger, happier."

"Thank you," Maggie said.

"Well, while we're toasting," Windsor said, "I guess this is as good a time as any to announce our news."

"Windsor," Grace said with a panicked look as she turned to face her husband.

"What? There's no reason not to tell them, is there?"

Maggie watched them with mounting apprehension.

Was Grace pregnant again? But that would be good news. And Grace wasn't acting like this was good news.

"I just..." Grace looked at Maggie and their eyes locked. "Maggie, I wanted to tell you alone."

"What in the world is it?" Maggie asked, looking from Grace to Windsor.

"Hey, this is some great toast!" Pijou said.

"Shut up, Pijou," Brigitte said. When Pijou looked at her sister, Brigitte shook her head. *Not now*, Brigitte mouthed.

"Well, it is good news," Windsor said, almost petulantly. "It's fantastic news. I've made a terrific coup. Remember that little computer company I was telling you about, Laurent? JP Electronics?"

Laurent nodded uncertainly.

"I bought it! Just yesterday."

Maggie looked at Grace. "The kicker, please," she said quietly.

"'Kicker'?" Marie asked, looking to René for translation.

"It's in Indiana," Grace said. "We're moving back home at the end of the summer."

4

"'We're moving back home,' she says. 'Pass the crème brulée.'"

Maggie straightened the duvet across their king-sized bed and then re-straightened it. She felt restless and fidgety. It was late and she was wide awake.

"They didn't serve *creme bruleé* tonight," Laurent said as he climbed into bed.

Maggie stopped straightening the duvet and eyed him suspiciously.

"You didn't know about this, did you?"

"No." Laurent closed his eyes. "The light please, *chérie.*"

Maggie got out of bed and went to the dresser. Her laptop was downstairs and probably uncharged. She rummaged in the top drawer and pulled out a notebook.

"I guess no time was really a good time to tell me," she said. "But it was a shock hearing it at like that in front of everyone."

She climbed back into bed.

"And I know she's not happy about it," she said, groping for a pencil on the bedside table. "I know she doesn't want to leave *St-Buvard*. It's Windsor who's insisting."

"The light, Maggie?"

"One minute. I mean, Grace *adores* France. She loves *St-Buvard*. I know she doesn't want to leave."

"Maggie, what are you doing?"

"I got a recipe from René that I want to get it down before I forget it."

"You are going to write it down from *memory?*" Laurent opened his eyes and peered at her as she wrote on the pad.

"It's very simple."

"You should have written it down at the party," Laurent said, punching his pillow.

"I remember the main bits."

"*Mon Dieu,*" he murmured, and closed his eyes.

"I thought Maggie took it very well, didn't you?" Windsor said. "She seemed very upbeat after we broke the news."

"It's a wonder."

"What? What's a wonder?"

"It's a wonder she didn't fling herself crying from the room the way you told her. 'Hey we're moving to Indiana. Get over it.'"

"I said nothing of the kind."

Grace looked at her husband from her dressing table, a frown creasing her perfect features.

"What made you blurt it out in front of fifty-two people at a dinner party for heaven's sake?"

"There were only ten people. Besides, I wasn't aware our moving stateside equated to being arrested for indecent exposure."

"I wanted to tell her first before she heard it like that."

"You've known for two weeks. Not my fault you're a coward."

Grace walked to the bed where Windsor was pulling off his shoes.

"I didn't know how to tell her," she said.

"Obviously."

Grace sat down next to him. She looked out their bedroom window into the inky outline of the forest that surrounded their home.

"I didn't know how to tell her without her realizing the truth."

Windsor tossed his keys into a dish on the dresser and returned to the bed. He sat down next to Grace.

"You mean, that you're ready to go home?"

Grace nodded sadly.

"Maggie still can't adjust to living here. How do you think she'd feel if she knew that St-Buvard wasn't *my* first choice as a permanent address either?"

Windsor took his wife's hand.

"You're a good friend, Grace, " he said, kissing her hand. "And I should know."

The olive grove was steeply terraced. The silver leaves of the gnarled and dark olive trees gave the grove a quiet elegance. Brigitte had deliberately chosen the spot for its remoteness—a good fifty kilometers from Nîmes, even further from Arles, and not a village or petrol station for five kilometers.

She spread the tablecloth out under the olive trees, wondering why she had bothered to iron it and knowing, of course, why she had. Thick bushes of hollyhocks and lavender bordered the picnic area. The strong scent of lavender boosted the ambiance.

She unpacked the picnic, looking up from time to time to see if she could see the approach of a car from down the terraced grove. She laid out a china dish of stuffed olives—dark and purple in their briny oil.

She placed a long baguette on the tablecloth next to a large bowl of radishes. Next to this, she set the *pissaladière*, a creamy onion tart dotted with anchovies and black olives.

She wiped her hands on a cloth napkin and frowned into the sun. It was hot. Really too hot for a picnic. But she couldn't bear the thought of meeting in a café somewhere, over drinks, over chipped ashtrays and pedestrian glances. It felt so much cleaner to meet here. Perhaps she would even relax a little bit.

She tucked her feet under her and took a deep breath. Perhaps the sweet scent of the lavender and the soft grass beneath her smartly pressed tablecloth would help her let go.

For one afternoon. For one hour.

Dr. Yves Genet climbed onto the nurse, brushing away her mild but nonetheless real protestations and labored briefly and noisily. When he finished, he pushed her away and dressed quickly. He chatted casually, even teasingly, with the woman—who was shaking and haltingly readjusting her clothing.

He stayed with her in the examination room long enough to inspect himself in the mirror for a razor burn on the side of his face, to comb his hair and to reposition the pens in the pocket of his white jacket and to smile gently at the nameless, nearly faceless nurse still seated on the examination table.

He squeezed her knee and left her to her inevitable tears.

Uncle August was the first to arrive. Brigitte could see his ancient Saab chugging up the hill and knew he would be charmed at the thought of conducting the interview outside in the blazing heat of a summer midday.

She looked at her *pissaladière* and hoped it wouldn't be too salty this time. She waved to him as he climbed out of his car and squinted up the terrace grove. Behind him, she could see a shiny black Mercedes snaking its way toward them.

She pulled her hand down and watched the large car as it pulled up beside Uncle August's Saab. She had wanted to make the introductions, but perhaps it was better this way. Maggie seemed a little intimidated by chefs in general, and after hearing his pedigree, by August Moreau in particular.

She watched as the figures of Grace and Maggie got out of the black Mercedes and after shaking hands with Uncle August began the climb up the hill.

"*Bonjour*, Brigitte!" Grace called to her. "We've brought the wine and your uncle too!"

Grace was really quite beautiful, Brigitte thought. Hers was an effortless beauty that appears thrown together but absolutely was not.

Maggie, on the other hand, had the more enduring looks. Her style was quirky and unsure and that suited her. She had a flawless complexion, too, which was unusual for someone in her thirties. It occurred to her as she watched Maggie's curtain of dark hair swinging against her shoulders that the American's dark eyes seemed to see a lot—for all her affect of insecurity.

"My God," Grace gasped as the three reached the picnic spot. "Is this some sort of trial? Because I'm terrible at aerobic sorts of things. Much better at cocktail sorts of things." She sank onto the picnic tablecloth, her linen skirt ballooning gently around her.

"Brigitte! I should have known you would pull a picnic out of the air! And such air! Ninety degrees!"

Uncle August kissed her and squeezed both of her hands

before turning his attention to the presentation of food on the tablecloth.

Brigitte welcomed Maggie and noticed how fresh and unfazed she appeared from the steep climb, and how her eyes sparkled with interest at the sight of the picnic spread.

Americans are like little children, Brigitte thought—always ready to be surprised and delighted.

"Maggie, *bonjour*," she said. "Ah, you have brought *le vin*, I see."

"It's from Laurent's stock," Maggie said, holding out two bottles.

"Excellent. Uncle August, have you tried it?"

"I have tried the *Domaine St-Buvard* label. Some of it is not bad." He smiled at Maggie.

"Don't worry, Maggie," Brigitte said, motioning her to sit down. "His bite is as boring as his bark." She turned to her uncle and wagged a finger. "Arf! Arf!"

"Brigitte, this is lovely!" Grace said. "The lavender, the beautiful flowers. A perfect spot for a picnic."

"I thought you might bring your children," Brigitte said, handing out small plates. "Or at least the baby."

"No, no," Grace said, as she spooned a few olives onto her plate. "It's Daddy's day to be with the children." She laughed. "He practically begged me to leave them home with him."

"Yeah, I'll bet," Maggie said, grinning. "What do you call this dish, Brigitte?"

"I call it olives and bread," Brigitte said, laughing. "Don't worry, Maggie, we will get into all that. But this is nothing." She waved a dismissive hand at the picnic. "Uncle August will tell you what true French food really is."

"Brigitte, you underrate yourself, as usual," August said gruffly. "True French food is simplicity itself. A crust of fresh bread, rubbed with a cut clove of garlic and dipped in the sweetest virgin olive oil. That is cooking at its most perfect, its most evolved."

Maggie pulled out a spiral notebook and a pen. "I guess the creams and butters and scallops and stuff gets tossed in later, huh?"

Everyone laughed.

Uncle August was a handsome, apple-faced man in his late sixties. His eyes were bright blue, his lips full. He had a full head of white hair which curled around the top of his collar.

"What is it you want to know, Madame Dernier?" August said as he lifted a wedge of the *pissaladière* onto his plate.

Maggie thought for a minute and looked uncertainly at Grace, who was cutting her own piece of onion tart and licking her fingers.

"I'm not really sure," she said. "I guess I thought I'd collect a bunch of local recipes?" She looked at Brigitte who smiled encouragingly at her.

"That seems like a good idea," Brigitte said.

"That is all you want from me?" August frowned.

"What else can you give me?" Maggie said. "I mean, what else is a cookbook but recipes?"

"Ahhh," August nodded as if finally satisfied with Maggie's answer. He took a bite of the pie and nodded again, this time at Brigitte.

"Excellent, Brigitte. Perfection." He quickly ate the rest of the piece and cut himself another.

"Yes, it's really delicious, Brigitte," Grace said, now fanning herself with a rolled up speeding ticket she had taken from her purse. "It's *pissaladière*, right?"

Maggie began to write. "How do you spell that?"

August reached over and put his heavy bronzed hand on top of her notepad.

"This will be much better," he said, breathing garlic and

onions into the warm air around Maggie's face, "if you take the notes after the experience. It's like making love, no? It spoils the mood to be jotting down tips while your lover is still tightly lodged..."

"Uncle August!" Brigitte winced.

"Ahh, yes, well, you understand, no?"

Grace burst out laughing, dropping her fan in the process.

"Perfectly," Maggie said and settled back for a very interesting lunch.

Later that evening, Maggie watched Laurent open a tin of goose *confit*, place the goose under the grill and sauté baby new potatoes in the goose fat. She prepared a green salad and brought up a chilled rosé from their basement.

For the first time in months, they worked together companionably and quietly to prepare their evening meal.

Maggie asked him no questions about the meal. She made no notations in her notebook. Laurent did not raise his voice or tune her out when she spoke. He did not appear to be shielding his activities at the stove or waiting for the phone to ring.

They sat down together at the dining room table and Maggie talked about her afternoon with Brigitte and Grace and she listened without rancor or resentment when Laurent told of his day in the vineyards with Jean-Luc.

It was a truly miraculous meal.

"And so you like Brigitte?" he asked.

"I do. She acted as if she'd known me for years."

"Perhaps she's in the market for a friend."

"What do you mean?"

"It sounds like she's chosen you to be her friend."

Maggie chewed thoughtfully and took a sip of the wine. It was still a bit tannic. She hadn't let it breathe long enough.

"You think she's in need of a friend?"

"She's married to a jerk."

"There is that."

They ate quietly for a moment.

"Is it possible she could help take the place of Grace for you?"

Maggie looked up from her dinner plate. It hadn't occurred to her that her crisis of losing Grace was an equal crisis for Laurent. In his mind, Grace helped make it bearable for Maggie in *St-Buvard*.

Without her, the pressure to leave France could become very heavy.

"Grace and I finally talked about her leaving," Maggie said. "She was sorry she hadn't told me sooner, blah blah blah. And where Windsor goes she must go too blah blah blah."

"What is this blah blah blah?"

"I guess it just doesn't sound like a very good reason to leave."

"Windsor's happiness, you mean?"

"What about Grace's happiness? Or the children's?"

Laurent pushed his empty dinner plate away. He stared into the bowl of his wine glass.

"So Grace is unhappy about leaving?" he said.

Maggie shrugged. "Not all that unhappy, I guess," she said.

"Grace wants to go too," Laurent said.

Maggie said nothing. Laurent poured more wine into her glass.

Laurent's hunting dog could be heard baying in the distance. It was a ghostly sound, painful and harsh in the otherwise still evening air.

"I wish you could have seen Brigitte today, Laurent," Maggie said. "She wasn't at all like she was the other night when Yves was there. She was relaxed and laughing. I've only known her a few days and yet I feel like she's going to be someone special in my life."

"I am very glad to hear this." Laurent smiled and then leaned across the table and kissed her. "I've missed you, *chérie*," he whispered into her ear.

She kissed him back and then moved to his side of the table where she slipped into his lap and put her arms around him. She kissed him deeply.

"That must have been a hell of a lunch," Laurent said nuzzling her neck and hair.

"I can't wait for you to meet August Moreau. He's already given me a lot of great ideas for the book." Maggie toyed with the long curls against Laurent's collar. "I've got Brigitte to thank for that too."

Laurent stood, still holding Maggie in his arms.

"I will thank each of them one by one for this incredible transformation," he said as he moved with her in his arms toward the staircase. "But first things first, as you Americans would say."

Marie stared out to the Roman gates of the city, lit up across the dark expanse of the Rhone. Two massive columns, each with a stone lion lounging on top, marked where the bridge had originally guarded the entrance to the city of Arles. Chills came whenever Marie imagined Roman soldiers directing the *Provençal* villagers of 400 AD to build the gates.

Tonight the gates looked sinister and malevolent in the dark and misty night.

"Do watch where you step, Marie. There's dog shit everywhere, " René said. He clucked softly to their little poodle and gave it a brisk tug on the leash.

"It's a beautiful night," Marie said, still looking at the river. She wore a heavy cotton *tablier* and she'd tucked her hair into a thin gauzy scarf. The evening breeze off the river gently flipped the wispy ties against her face.

"As long as one holds one's nose," René said.

Marie tucked her hand into the pocket of René's cardigan. "Brigitte called today," she said.

"Yes? Everything is well?"

"She had a picnic with August and Grace."

"Oh, yes, I remember they talked about it at the dinner party. How was it? Everyone have a good time? *Genvieve!* Stop that you naughty dog! Little beast would roll in the muck if we let her."

"She's a dog, after all."

"Anything else?"

"Seemed she felt a special connection with Grace's friend, Maggie."

"You are disappointed it was not Grace."

Marie laughed. "How well you know me! I know it's silly, but since I've come to care so much for Grace, I thought the two of them might hit it off. And I've found so many similarities between them."

"Maggie seemed very nice."

"Yes, of course," Marie said impatiently. "And I'm delighted Brigitte wants to pursue a friendship with her."

"Especially with your darling Grace about to piss off back to the U.S."

"René!"

"Well? Am I wrong? Some friend! *Genvieve!* No!"

"She hadn't even told Maggie that she was leaving. You could see what a shock it was to her." Marie shook her head.

"And to you."

"Yes. And to me." Marie shoved both her hands into the pockets of her *tablier*. "But no one could see that."

"Because no one was looking but me, of course."

Marie smiled at him.

"And that bastard, Yves?" René said. "Did Brigitte mention where that scumbag was tonight? I assume he was not at home."

"Working late at the hospital."

"How I would like to murder that jerk!"

"It doesn't help, René."

"It helps *me*. Just thinking of the bastard lying in a pool of his own gore helps me quite a bit! Why don't they just divorce?"

"You know why."

"Even if she's miserable, Marie? You would have our Brigitte stay in a marriage of pain and degradation?"

"She is married to him. She made a vow before God."

"Why would a loving God bless such a union? Why would he want our Brigitte to be miserable?"

"Don't you think it hurts me to see her like this?" Marie turned to face her husband. "She is Catholic. *We*, in case I must remind you, are Catholic."

"This, about being Catholic, I do not accept," René said stubbornly.

"It doesn't work that way, René."

"It works that way for me."

"Because you are a man." Marie's voice softened and she put her hand back into his pocket. "Woman was created to remind you of the rules. Now, come, bring that bad dog away from the wall. She's done enough damage. Let's go home."

"Brigitte could move back home into her old bedroom. Wouldn't that be wonderful?"

"Yes, my dear. It truly would." Marie called to the little dog and they left the damp parapet and began the long, winding walk through the quiet cobblestone streets to their apartment.

～

Early the next morning, Marie was awakened by René

returning to their bedroom with a cup of coffee for her and the quiet announcement that there were four policemen downstairs.

Late the night before, their daughter Brigitte had been brutally murdered.

5

L aurent had gone off earlier that morning to finish the repair work on the stone walls around the vineyard. Determined to be as involved with her own project as he was with his, Maggie waved him off after breakfast and turned once more to her laptop notes and recipes.

To her surprise, an hour of working at the breakfast table in their sunny kitchen passed quickly. She pulled to the top of her pile those recipes dictated by Uncle August and decided to use them as the core of her book.

They were basic recipes, exemplifying what August called "farmhouse cooking." The simplicity of the recipes, combined with their complex tastes and versatility, gave Maggie the new angle for the book she had been looking for.

Feeling happy with her morning's work, Maggie allowed herself a small break to walk through the garden and cut some sunflowers. Back in the kitchen with the flowers, she was arranging them in a vase when she saw a police car pull up onto the gravel drive of the *mas.*

Two men got out—one in uniform and the other in a suit. Maggie dried her hands and went to open the front door.

"Madame Dernier?" said the man in the suit. He was a handsome man of thirty something of average height with clear blue eyes, dark hair and a tidy mustache over a full, sensuous mouth.

"Is Laurent all right? Has he been hurt?"

"Your husband? No, Madame, he is fine."

"Oh thank goodness. Come in, please," she said. They followed her into the living room.

"I am Detective Inspector Roger Bedard, and this is Sergeant Michaud." The detective presented his identification.

Maggie remembered the detective from the tragedy at Domaine St-Buvard a couple of years ago. She'd not spoken to him then however.

Bedard sat on the sofa and Maggie sat facing him. His sergeant remained standing. Her hands felt damp, even though she still held the kitchen towel.

"What's this all about?"

"I regret to inform you that the body of Madame Brigitte Genet was discovered last night on the side of the A-24 at approximately two this morning."

Maggie put her hand to her mouth and felt the horror of his words sink in.

"I am told that you were friends with Madame Genet?"

Maggie nodded numbly.

"You saw Madame Genet yesterday, I believe?"

Maggie tried to piece together what she was hearing.

"How did she die? Was it a car accident?"

Bedard pressed down the hairs of his mustache with a well-manicured hand.

"It was not a road accident, no," he said.

"An accident *how* then?"

"We are not thinking it *was* an accident," Bedard replied, watching Maggie carefully.

Maggie felt the hairs on the back of her neck begin to tingle.

Not an accident?

"Madame Genet was discovered by a family of German tourists," Bedard said as he pulled a notebook out of his jacket pocket. "She was nude upon discovery."

Maggie shook her head.

It can't be. Murder? I just saw her yesterday!

"We are hoping that you may help us reconstruct some of her last day...before she died."

The kindness in his voice finally provoked Maggie to give in to the emotion that had been building up inside her.

"I cannot believe this," she said, her hand still covering her mouth and surprised at the intensity of her feelings. "I just can't believe this."

An hour later, Maggie stood at the end of the Domaine St-Buvard gravel drive waiting for Grace. The police had asked for Maggie's description of the afternoon spent with Brigitte, had thanked her for her help, and then disappeared into the harsh Provençal sunlight.

Within minutes, Maggie was on the phone to Grace, who was in the middle of her own visit from the police.

Twenty minutes later, Grace's shiny black Mercedes appeared around the sharp bend that led over the stone bridge Maggie's farmhouse.

"Did you leave a note for Laurent?" Grace asked as she turned the car around in the driveway.

"I did. Are you okay?"

"I'm fine. I just want to get there and do whatever we can to help."

Maggie winced as Grace narrowly missed a row of garbage cans on the side of the road.

"What did the cops tell you?" Grace asked. "Did they tell you how she died?"

"Not really," Maggie said.

"They told me, or rather, they told Windsor and he told me. Brigitte was raped and then had her brains bashed out."

Maggie stared at Grace's profile. "What's the matter with you, Grace?"

A look of astonishment passed across Grace's face.

"What are you talking about? I'm only saying what the police told Win!"

"Well, can you at least have the decency to act a little revolted," Maggie said. "That might come in handy before you go and try to console her bereaved mother."

Grace slammed the brakes and pulled the car onto the road shoulder. She twisted in her seat to face Maggie.

"I am every bit as horrified as you, Maggie Newberry Dernier, and how dare you intimate I am not."

"I *will* intimate it and you'd better get a grip, Grace, before you try to act out a charade that even I can tell is false."

Grace stared angrily at her for a moment, and then turned back to face the steering wheel.

A moment passed.

"She was going to be my replacement," Grace said. "That's why you're taking it so hard."

"That's a horrible thing to say," Maggie said.

But true. And she was now angry at herself as well as Grace.

"I know. I'm sorry," Grace said. "I didn't feel the connection with her that you did. I saw it yesterday and I was amazed. I even went home and told Win, 'Wow, Maggie's over me already. Found someone she's going to be best friends with. Out with the old, etcetera etcetera.' Look, I didn't know her hardly at all. I'd only met her twice, same as you. How can I act like I'm going to miss her?"

"Forget it, Grace. The only thing that matters now is

Marie. If you think you can help her then concentrate on that. But don't be so flippant about how she died. It's offensive."

Grace pulled the car back onto the road.

"Wow, a manners lesson from Maggie Newberry," she said. "We really are coming to the end of our days, aren't we?"

The scene at Marie and René's house was mayhem. The police had set up a temporary headquarters in the middle of Marie's salon.

Seven policemen alternately talked and joked amongst themselves and questioned René. They had made themselves at home with the coffeemaker in the kitchen.

When Maggie entered the house, she immediately encountered René, who was waving his arms dramatically and shouting.

"I will kill the bastard! Why don't you have him in custody? It's her husband, you idiots! You want his address? Can I give you a lift to his place? What are you doing here?"

Marie sat weeping in the main salon. Wondering why she wasn't upstairs in her room, Maggie hurried over to her. She put a hand on the older woman's shoulder and squeezed it. Marie only moaned.

"Marie, we're here," Maggie said. She motioned to Grace who was still standing in the doorway.

"Grace, come sit with her, will you? I'm going to get her a drink."

Marie looked up into Maggie's face. Maggie nearly recoiled at the expression of naked pain.

Grace sat down next to Marie and put her arm around her.

"I'm here, darling."

When Maggie entered the kitchen, Detective Inspector Bedard was speaking to a group of uniformed policemen.

"Medoin, you need to get Pernon out of the house during the search. "

Bedard nodded to Maggie then raised an eyebrow.

"Sorry to interrupt," she said. "I'm looking for water or coffee for Madame Pernon."

Bedard snapped his fingers and a young uniformed man began to fill the coffeemaker with water.

"You are here to console Madame?"

"We are friends of the family," Maggie said firmly.

"Perhaps there is a better time to pay your respects," Bedard said, his blue eyes never wavering from Maggie's.

A phone rang somewhere in the house and was promptly answered. Maggie could hear René's raving begin to descend to a lower decibel. Marie's sobbing was now audible.

"Perhaps there is a better time to ask your questions," Maggie said, glaring back at Bedard.

I won't be bullied into not helping when I'm needed.

As if reading her thoughts, Bedard waved his men out of the kitchen and turned to her.

"It's never a good time to do my job when there is a death. She has lost her daughter. A precious treasure. I have such a treasure. But in a situation like this, the early minutes of the investigation are the most important."

"You have a child?"

As soon as Maggie spoke the words, she felt an electric shock tingle up through her fingers and hands. It was a personal question to an unquestionably attractive man.

And it instantly revealed the attraction to him that she had not been consciously aware of before. She realized that as soon as Bedard revealed a single personal comment about himself as he just had, the two of them would move—even if only by the narrowest margin—into a less than professional relationship.

The thought surprised and unnerved her.

"A two-year old daughter," he said softly. "It is unavoidable to imagine how I might feel if the words I spoke to Madame Pernod today were ever spoken to me. And I cannot allow myself to imagine it if I am to do my job." He smiled sadly at Maggie.

He feels it too. Of course he does. Something happened between us for God's sake and now I've got to shake it off and do what's necessary.

In a million years she never would have expected to feel this *today* of all days.

She cleared her throat, no longer able to look at him.

"Do what you need to. But please let me stay and give comfort if I can."

"Of course."

That evening Laurent spooned up a plateful of steaming *ratatouille* and set it down before Maggie.

"You were gone a long time," he said.

Maggie opened her napkin onto her lap.

"I couldn't leave until Grace was ready to."

"Madame Pernon is badly shaken?"

"Of course."

Laurent settled himself in his chair, then picked up his wine glass and studied the blood red liquid. His face was set and somber.

"When is the funeral?"

"The police are releasing the body this weekend. It was really horrible, Laurent. I mean, René was screaming at one end of the house and Marie was crying at the other and all these cops were milling about and the phone was ringing constantly. Plus, all the police were drinking coffee so if they weren't all edgy *before*, they were totally hopped-up eventually."

Maggie took a sip of her wine. "This is good. Is it one of ours?"

Laurent shook his head.

"Anyway, so it went on like that pretty much the whole afternoon. Then Pijou came home and she was yelling at the cops. I'm really not sure why. My French isn't that good. And of course, René was yelling at the cops telling them that Yves was the murderer. "

"René accused Yves?"

"Hell, yes. And then Pijou—she must've been drunk or something—chose that moment to accuse Marie of liking Brigitte best."

"*Incroyable.*" Laurent shook his head.

"It was a circus," Maggie said. "I felt so bad for Marie. She was just destroyed. Well, naturally."

"Naturally."

Maggie got up with her plate.

"You are finished?"

"Look, I'm sorry, Laurent. But I've had a pretty emotional afternoon and I guess I'm not all that hungry."

She put the plate back down on the table and came over to him. Quietly she slipped into his lap and he put his arms around her.

"I don't know what's wrong with me."

"*Ça ne fait rien,*" Laurent said softly. "Why did the police visit you, do you think?"

"Because of the picnic. Grace and I were one of the last ones to see Brigitte alive."

"It is a very sad thing,"

Maggie pulled away. "I think I want to be part of helping find the person who did this."

"The police are doing what they can in this investigation," Laurent said. He reached past Maggie for his wine glass. She got up from his lap and sat down again next to him.

"And I want to help."

Laurent seemed more interested in looking at the colors of the wine in his glass at first.

"I suppose violence and death are more interesting than writing cookbooks," he said finally. This was a reference to the murder of their mutual friend the year before when Maggie had investigated and tracked down his murderer.

"I was thinking of doing both," she said. "The cookbook, too."

"What is the name of the man in charge of the case?"

"Roger Bedard," Maggie said. "Do you know him?"

Laurent's nefarious past had more than once thrown an interesting coincidence into Maggie's life.

He shook his head.

A silence bloomed between them for a few beats before Laurent spoke.

"You must do what you must do. I am being supportive of you, of course, *chérie.*"

Maggie felt a flush of affection toward her husband. She leaned over and kissed him on the lips.

"You're planning on being up early tomorrow," she said. "And now it looks like I've got a reason to be, too. Let's go to bed."

The restraining wall of rough-hewn stones marked off the little patio and tables from the surrounding lawn. The plane trees that lined the road leading to *St-Buvard* grouped around the bar's terrace in a friendly huddle, spilling their large leaves onto the pink-stoned pavers and the wrought-iron tables and chairs.

Le Canard was the only café in the village. In such a small village, the little restaurant served the important function of disseminating news and gossip, providing delicious fare to accompany the many excellent wines of the region, and affording a nice view of the ancient stone fountain in the village center.

With the *boulangerie* closed and the post office open only two days a week, the café was rivaled only by the *charcuterie* for business.

Maggie had spent many afternoons at *Le Canard* in her two years in St-Buvard. It was a favorite place to catch a bite to eat with Laurent and was the first place she looked for him when she couldn't find him in the vineyard. She and Grace had taken to spending a pleasant hour each week on *Le Canard's* terrace too.

Detective Inspector Bedard had suggested they meet at *Le Canard* when Maggie called him.

He was sitting with her now at a patio table. He lit a cigarette and pushed his demitasse cup away from the ashtray. His eyes looked more gray than blue in this light. His complexion was clear and unmarked.

She had decided at some point in the night that any attraction she felt for this man was simply not worthy of consideration. She would not let it deter her from her interest in Brigitte's murder or threaten her love for Laurent.

And so, if it didn't threaten her marriage, why not recognize the attraction, at least to herself? Why not enjoy the feeling of Bedard's eyes as he watched her? Why not? To lie to herself about it would only encourage a guilt she hadn't earned.

Armed with this sound logic and a new self-awareness, Maggie allowed herself to relax in the company of this handsome man.

"I won't get in your way," Maggie said.

"I know. I won't allow it."

"But I can be a help."

"I cannot imagine how, Madame Dernier." Bedard smiled and exhaled a thin stream of smoke out of the side of his mouth. "You are asking for facts on a case my department has deemed confidential."

Maggie leaned across the table earnestly.

"All I'm asking for is information that will be public record sooner or later."

"I am sorry, Madame."

"Call me 'Maggie, please,'" Maggie said, leaning back.

He raised an eyebrow at that but said nothing.

Maggie felt a desire to throw him off balance. "Are you divorced?" she asked.

The Frenchman's smile turned into an outright grin.

"I am Catholic," he said. "I do not believe in it."

"Right," Maggie said briskly.

It irritated her that the man would flirt with her—and that was without mistake what he was doing right this very minute—while he was still married. The fact that she, a married woman, had responded, if ever so slightly, to his attentions didn't seem as deliberate a misdemeanor somehow.

"No, not divorced," Bedard said. "Widowed."

Oh, God. I should get up and run like hell right now.

"I'm sorry," Maggie said, wadding up a paper napkin in her embarrassment.

"In any event, I must get back to the station," he said, clearly enjoying her discomfort and standing up. "It should hearten you to know that my men and I have many leads and we are confident about solving this case quickly."

He signaled for the waiter and took out his wallet.

"Is Yves one of the leads?" she asked.

Bedard squinted into the sun as if trying to read one of the tree limbs.

"We are questioning everyone. I'm sorry I could not help you, Maggie. I understand you want to do something for your friend."

He paid the bill and, smiling at her in a way that Maggie would definitely describe as *meaningfully,* left.

The waiter returned and Maggie ordered another coffee. The late afternoon sun had descended behind the tops of the trees and she felt a cool breeze as it blew through the outdoor café.

The summer had been so brutal, and autumn had seemed like it would never come. But, sitting there in the dying sunlight, Maggie could sense the evolving seasons, and knew that a dramatic change was imminent.

An hour later, after parking her Citroën in the driveway of *Domaine St-Buvard*, Maggie noticed an old Renault with a dented fender parked in the drive. She looked into the Renault on her way to the front door.

A chartreuse cardigan was wadded up in the passenger seat. Maggie could see the Versace label clearly. *Who the hell?*

As she walked through the front door, she heard voices from the kitchen. A bubble of girlish coquettishness mixed with the solid rumble of Laurent's slow, calm French.

This is reason enough to learn the damn language, Maggie thought as she tossed down her purse and walked into the kitchen.

Pijou Pernon sat on a stool against one of the counters next to Laurent, who stood with his back to Maggie as he chopped garlic on a wooden chopping board. Pijou was drinking a large glass of red wine and wearing something one might feel embarrassed to wear on a topless beach.

When Pijou turned to look at Maggie, her expression of fawning attentiveness did not waver.

Maggie was sure she must be drunk.

"*Bonjour*, Pijou," Maggie said as she came into the kitchen.

Laurent swung around to see her.

"*Allo*, you are back," he said and they kissed briefly before he resumed his chopping.

"How is your mother?" Maggie asked.

Pijou rolled her eyes and nudged Laurent's big beefy shoulder.

"You see? It's always about Brigitte. Honest to God, this must be the ultimate one upsmanship ever!"

Laurent turned to Maggie, who was staring at Pijou in horror.

"She is very upset, Maggie. I am making food for us."

The Frenchman's version of a soothing cup of tea, Maggie thought. A heady dollop of *aïoli* with hard-boiled eggs and boiled white potatoes.

What could they not cure?

"Good idea," Maggie said. "Is there any more wine?"

"Stupid question," Laurent muttered good-naturedly as he wiped his hands on a kitchen towel and poured her a glass. "What did Bedard have to say, eh?"

"Bedard? You talked to him?" Pijou smeared a streak of black mascara down her face and Maggie saw that she had been crying. "God, isn't he gorgeous? Of course, *Maman* and *Papa* both hate him. They think he is the devil. He's not arrested Yves yet and he hasn't fallen all over them as if they're bereaved royalty or something. In fact, René thinks Bedard suspects *them*. Can you believe it?" She laughed roughly. "They are so stupid!"

Maggie looked at Laurent but he had turned back to his chopping board.

Pijou jabbed Maggie with a long finger.

"So what did Bedard tell you? Did he tell you he thinks René did it? Is he going to pick up Yves? Is he going to take me up on my offer?" She grinned at Maggie. "I don't suppose he mentioned me?"

"He wouldn't tell me anything," Maggie said. "He wants me to stay out of things."

Laurent glanced at her over his shoulder. *Sorry.*

Maggie turned back to Pijou. "Is the funeral Saturday?"

Pijou nodded and slid off her stool to stand, unsteadily, against the kitchen counter. "You know who I think did it?" she said. "Brigitte's best friend."

"Who would that be?" Maggie asked. *With or without Bedard's approval*, she thought, *I'm on the case.*

"Madeleine Dupré? You know her?"

Maggie shook her head. "Were they friends a long time?"

"A very long time. Madeleine's husband works with Yves. Doctors' wives. That's how they know each other. Madeleine was banging Yves on a regular basis until Brigitte found out. Put a dent in the friendship but, darling, they still lunched regularly, you know. They certainly weren't going to be tacky about it."

Maggie watched Pijou carefully to determine how drunk she was.

"Yves slept with Brigitte's best friend?"

"Oh, yes." Pijou smirked. "Does that shock you, Madame Dernier?"

"I suppose even more shocking is the idea that they remained friends afterward."

"None of us is really sure about that." Pijou said and spilled her wine on the counter.

"Don't worry about it," Maggie said, although Pijou didn't look she cared one way or the other. "Do you think Brigitte knew that they continued to sleep together?"

"Well, you know Yves," Pijou said, shrugging. She seemed to be coming down from her earlier high.

"Not really," Maggie said. "But I guess the general opinion is that he's a real rotter, huh?"

Pijou pushed her wineglass away on the counter and put a hand to her head.

Looks like we'll be dining alone, after all.

"Has anyone talked to Madeleine since Brigitte's murder?" Maggie asked.

"Huh? Well, I certainly haven't," Pijou said with a sarcastic tone. "I mean I would hardly talk to her, would I?"

Maggie took a chance. "Why not?"

"Because of the jealousy thing, stupid!"

Laurent turned to watch the women and Maggie signaled him not to interrupt.

"Meaning Madeleine was jealous of you?"

"Of course."

"And that would be because why exactly?"

"That would be," Pijou said smugly, "because I was Yves' lover too."

6

I t rained the morning of the funeral which was held at the
Church of Saint-Trophime in Arles. Afterwards, the
funeral procession wound its way through the narrow,
cobblestone streets to a nearby black hearse.

Maggie and Laurent walked with Grace and Windsor at the
tail of the solemn group of mourners.

"Looks like mostly business associates," Grace said. She
looked impeccable in a dark Prada suit. She wore a dazzling
ten-carat diamond and gold bracelet on her black-gloved
hands.

"Whose?" Maggie asked.

"Yves, naturally," Grace answered with raised eyebrows.

Yves smiled broadly and clapped a man heartily on the
shoulder.

*He's acting like he's with pals on the golf course and not at his
murdered wife's funeral.*

Maggie watched René throughout the funeral service. He
was more focused on Yves than on what was happening at the
altar. Marie sat next to him, her shoulders hunched and
shaking with sobs.

"Yves' alibi is that he was in surgery at the time," Grace said. "And I guess it's a pretty good one since no less than nine people can verify it."

"Wow," Maggie said.

"He really looks cut up, doesn't he?"

"Do you know which one's Madeleine?" Maggie whispered as they walked behind the procession.

Grace scanned the crowd.

"The one in the chartreuse Versace dress. Talk about bad taste."

Maggie shrugged. She knew little about fashion. "It's a pretty dress."

"To a *funeral*?" Grace said in disbelief.

Madeleine wore sunglasses. Her blonde hair was tucked elegantly into a silk scarf. Her cheekbones gave promise to the beauty behind the glasses. She held tightly to the arm of a tall, brown-haired man.

He had a nice face, Maggie thought, and she wondered if he was aware of his wife's adventures.

"I heard she was Yves's lover," Grace said. "Pijou told me."

"Marie's still pretty shook up," Maggie said, changing the subject.

"She breaks my heart. I hope they find the monster who did this soon."

When they arrived at the cemetery, they could see that only a smaller number of mourners were gathered under umbrellas in the warm drizzle beside the open grave.

Marie and René stood together holding each other. They looked stunned.

Yves was not there.

"The bastard!" Grace hissed in a whisper when they drew closer.

"He can't make you happy, Grace," Windsor said. "He's a bastard for being here and a bastard for not."

"He can't finish out the funeral for his own wife? Incredible."

Maggie spotted Bedard standing alone at a distance from the rest of the group. Their eyes met and he nodded. Maggie thought his eyebrows rose just a tad at the sight of her tall, handsome husband.

"Is that Bedard?" Laurent asked.

"Yes. I guess he's checking to see if somebody new shows up. Or maybe if there's going to be any graveside confessions or theatrics."

"He's good-looking."

"If you say so."

The rain was coming down harder now and they huddled under Windsor's oversized golf umbrella. Grace had scolded him for bringing it because of the large Sunkist logo emblazoned across its top, but Maggie was grateful for its size.

As the priest began the last words for Brigitte, Maggie could hear Marie's muted sobs under the sound of the rain. The priest's voice droned on and so did Marie's moans.

Maggie looked at Brigitte's coffin and tried to remember the woman inside. She tried to remember Brigitte's smile, her coy affection with Uncle August, her instant mutual heartfelt connection with Maggie.

The next week, Maggie drove to the restaurant in Aix recommended to her by Uncle August. She normally loved to spend time in Aix and shopped there frequently with Grace. Today, as she drove into town, she reminded herself that this was the way it was going to be from now on.

Her, alone, without Grace.

Further conversations with Grace on the subject of her leaving had only proved frustrating. Grace had been enigmatic about her feelings on leaving *St-Buvard*. Maggie knew she *wanted* to go.

Before it had always been *Maggie* who was unable to reconcile herself to a foreign land. It was always *Maggie* resistant to try the new foods, adapt to the customs, learn the language. Grace was the one comfortable in her castle in the French countryside like she'd been born there.

But now Grace was leaving all the foreignness behind for a tract mansion in a Midwestern subdivision—complete with chain grocery stores down the street and perfectly understandable television every night.

Grace was leaving a life that made you work so hard for just a very little payoff, for a life that put you to sleep.

This last thought surprised Maggie. Up until now she would have believed that the better life was in America—*anywhere* in America. But now that she was faced with watching her support system fly first-class back home to the States, she wasn't so sure.

Sure, it was comfortable and easy there. *But, maybe*, Maggie found herself thinking, *I'm a little young for it to be so easy just yet. Maybe I can reserve that for my old age and, for now, take my adventures a little on the more complicated side.*

Buoyed with this idea, Maggie swung into the restaurant, *La Bonne Idee* and, with a confidence she hadn't felt in months, asked the *maître d'* for the owner and chef.

May God forgive me and have mercy on me. Finally, forgive me for the terrible crimes I have committed.

Marie felt the pain shoot up into her hips from her knees but would not shift her position to relieve the agony. She had been kneeling in the empty church for nearly three hours, her head pressed against the prayer bench in front of her, her hands squeezed in a tight clasp at her chest.

Have you left me, Lord? When I have defended this marriage to everyone? You knew, my God, you allowed, the monstrosities to occur within that union. Why is this your answer to me? You let her live in agony, you allowed her to die brutally. And you still demand my love. Who are you? Who are you? And who have you helped me to become?

The tears flowed again with Marie's sobs echoing up to the top of the ancient rafters.

～

"So, you're saying it's all in the wrist?" Maggie scribbled down everything the man was saying to her and wished she'd brought a tape recorder.

The great chef shrugged. "You must have the right ingredients, of course."

Maggie smiled thinly at him. *What an ass.*

"But the secret to the perfect omelet," she said, still writing. "Is that after one has assembled the right ingredients, you fold the eggs by using short, sharp jerks of the omelet pan."

"More or less."

Maggie closed her notebook. "You've been a great help. I must thank Monsieur Moreau for this introduction."

The restaurateur did not respond.

"I will, of course, reference and source every contributor to my book," Maggie said, trying to remember where the exit was past the maze of tables. "And your restaurant, too."

The man shrugged.

"Well," Maggie said as she got to her feet and extended her hand, "Thanks again and you can kiss my ass, Monsieur."

The man stood but with a look of astonishment.

"It's an American idiom," Maggie said. "I hope it translated okay. My French isn't very good."

"Of course," the man said, watching Maggie with unsure eyes now. "I will show you out."

"Awesome."

Once on the street outside, Maggie jammed her notebook into her bag and let out a loud sigh. The man had been cold and egotistical from the start. He was totally convinced that Maggie would somehow winkle his precious recipes from him and thereby ensure the collapse of his restaurant empire.

What a waste of time.

Not eager to drive back to *Domaine St-Buvard* so soon, she settled in at a nearby café and ordered a tall *café crème*. She pulled out her notebook and scanned her notes. It was around four o'clock on a Tuesday afternoon and the café and the nearby street were busy.

Maggie enjoyed the noise and the movement. When her coffee came, she sank back into her chair and just let the hum of her surroundings engulf her.

She thought of Laurent and how loving he had been last night. They still hadn't had a fight and it had been over a week. She made a point to stop herself from observing him too closely in the kitchen while he cooked or complaining about the time he spent in the vineyard.

Suddenly Maggie saw someone she recognized.

Madeleine Dupré wore a pale lavender jogging suit with gold slippers. *Only she was definitely not going jogging.* A large black patent leather shopping bag hung from one shoulder as she sauntered past.

Without thinking, Maggie threw down the money for her coffee, gathered up her purse and notes, and followed her. Surprised at how easily she could keep Madeleine in view without being detected, Maggie kept a good distance between them.

Madeleine stopped briefly to look at a strawberry vendor's selection but turned away without buying. She walked to the end of the street, then turned up a tree-lined avenue with elegant apartments fronting both sides. Maggie paused at a kiosk selling original watercolors of Provençal street life and watched Madeleine hurry up the first set of stone steps and disappear behind the glossy double doors of the nearest apartment building.

Bedard never said I couldn't talk to people.

She looked up at the street-facing balcony and saw the French doors open and Madeleine emerge onto the balcony. She was smoking a cigarette and seemed to be talking to someone.

Cautiously, Maggie crossed the street and entered the apartment building. Inside, the foyer was lined with glossy wood paneling and a line of brass mailboxes with glittering nameplates.

There was only one nameplate that featured the word *Docteur.*

Before she could lose her nerve, Maggie climbed the stairs to the first landing and rapped on the door. Within seconds, it was opened to reveal the homely, kind-faced man that had been with Madeleine at the funeral. He smiled at Maggie.

"*Oui?*"

She had forgotten about the language thing. *What if he doesn't speak English?*

"Dr. Dupré?" Maggie said. Over his shoulder she could see Madeleine on the balcony. "My name is Maggie Dernier. I don't suppose you speak English?"

The man grinned and Maggie felt herself relax.

"A little, yes," he said. "But my wife, she is very much better, I think, Madame Dernier." He opened the door and invited her inside the apartment.

"Oh, thank you," Maggie said, stepping onto a hand-made

Aubusson Chinese rug. She caught her image in a large gilt-framed oval mirror hanging in the foyer. "I am—was—a friend of Brigitte's and I saw you and Madame Dupré at the funeral on Saturday."

"*Qui est-ce, Richard?*" Madeleine said as she stepped inside off the balcony.

Maggie was able to see her clearly for the first time. She looked like a cross between Grace Kelley and Cybil Shepherd, Maggie thought. Gorgeous in a pale, wispy blonde sort of way.

I'd need Grace here to confirm it but I think Madeleine has had a little work done.

"A friend of Brigitte's, *chérie,*" her husband responded, then ushered Maggie into the sunny salon.

"Brigitte?" Madeleine frowned and extended her hand to Maggie. "You are *Americaine,* yes?"

"Yes," Maggie said. "I know you must think this is strange but I just needed to talk to someone who knew Brigitte really well, and her folks are still just so upset."

"Please sit down," Madeleine said, still holding Maggie's hand. "I am so glad you have come. So glad to meet another friend of Brigitte's."

Maggie could see tears glittering in Madeleine's eyes.

"And I am very happy to be leaving my wife in your care," Richard said as he picked up his lab coat. "She is needing to talk, I think, and your visit is right away the good thing."

He looked at Madeleine with a *have I got that right?* sort of look and both women burst out laughing in spite of themselves.

"My English is being very bad," he said.

Maggie couldn't help noticing the man's loving attention to his wife, which reminded her of how Laurent used to respond to Maggie.

"No, it's great," Maggie said. "You should get an earful of my French."

Richard kissed his wife. "I must be at the hospital," he said. "I am hoping to see you again, Madame Dernier."

I hope so too, Maggie thought. Something about him made her think the doctor would get along wonderfully with her own great bear of a Frenchman.

After he left Maggie began again with Madeleine.

"I'm sorry to just barge in on you like this," Maggie said.

"I'm glad you did. There is no one who knew Brigitte as I did. Not her ratty little sister—I'm sorry, are you friends with Pijou?"

Maggie laughed. "Not really."

"Good." Madeleine grinned. "It would definitely stand in the way of our being very close."

"Tell me about Brigitte," Maggie said. "I didn't really get to know her. And now that she's gone, I'm missing her more than makes sense."

Madeleine nodded and her tears were back.

"It makes sense to me. Brigitte had a way about her. She could make you love her and trust her almost immediately. It worked better with women, strangely enough. Even though Brigitte was, of course, quite beautiful. Her vital connections, if I can call them that, were always stronger with women."

"Except with her own sister."

Madeleine frowned.

"Pijou is a pig. Maybe it was just jealousy, you know? Brigitte had such magnetism and Pijou, well, magnetism is not something she has."

"How did you come to know Brigitte?"

"Through Richard's association with Yves. They worked together. Sooner or later, we all started going out."

Maggie tried to detect any special inflection when Madeleine mentioned Yves' name, but couldn't.

"Was Brigitte happy, do you think?"

For the first time, Madeleine gave Maggie a mildly suspicious look.

I'm going too fast.

"Happy, when?" Madeleine asked. She leaned over and offered Maggie a cigarette.

"No thanks. You know, in her life. Generally. In her marriage. I know nothing about Yves."

Madeleine lit her cigarette. "What is it you want to know, Madame Dernier?"

Crap.

"Please. Call me Maggie."

"Okay."

"I want to help the police find out who did this to Brigitte."

"You are working with the police?"

"No. They asked me to butt out."

Madeleine frowned. "I don't understand."

"They don't want me to do what I am doing. I think I can assist them. But I need your help."

Madeleine exhaled a sliver of blue smoke. "I'll tell you what I can."

"*Merci.* Have you talked to the police yet?"

Madeleine's frown deepened. It looked unnatural, Maggie thought. Like Saran Wrap stretched across a too-large bowl. Either the facelift was recent or the surgeon had tried to take a few too many years off.

"Richard talked to them on my behalf," Madeleine said. "I was too upset at first and they haven't been back."

"Was Yves bashing Brigitte around? I mean, that's what I hear and you'd know if it's true."

Madeleine ground out her cigarette. "Yes, of course it's true. He beat her."

"She must have talked to you about it."

"Not really."

"No? She didn't talk about it? I mean, she'd come to lunch

or something and have all these bruises, maybe a black eye and you wouldn't mention it?"

Madeleine stared outside as if visualizing the scene Maggie had painted.

"Yes. That's right."

"Did she ever talk about Yves?"

"In what way?"

"You know, Madeleine. In a *I'm unhappy and he's beating me up* kind of way. You know, the kind of thing a battered wife might say about the bastard who's hurting her."

"She didn't talk about Yves at all."

"Really? That's kind of weird, isn't it?"

Madeleine reached into her purse and withdrew a gold tube of lipstick to replace the lipstick she'd smoked off. Maggie noticed the brand: Clarins. Expensive. Very French.

"Is it?" Madeleine said.

"Well, think about it. I mean, imagine your own husband. You talk about *him*, don't you?"

Madeleine smiled briefly. "That's different."

"In what way?"

"I love my husband and, like many women, I enjoy trading stories about him with other women. But Brigitte hated Yves. What was there for her to say? *Oh, he smacked me a good one this morning?*"

"It must have killed you to see her treated like that," Maggie said.

Madeleine let out a big sigh. "She was my friend. And I loved her."

Sometimes, it's all very simple, Maggie thought. She leaned over to put her hand on top of Madeleine's and was surprised when the Frenchwomen responded by putting her arms around her. The two women sat quietly for a moment before Madeleine pulled away.

"I suppose you know I slept with him. I cannot imagine that *cochon* Pijou keeping the information to herself."

"I guess I was hoping it was a lie."

"How I wish I could say it was. Don't try to imagine how I could do such a thing—to Brigitte, to Richard."

"Did the affair last very long?"

"Affair? There was no affair. It was a, how do you Americans say it? A quickie?" She laughed. "One time, never again."

"Does Richard know?"

"Thank God, no. It would hurt him terribly. Although the idiot would forgive us both a hundred times over. He actually likes Yves." She shook her head. "What a mess. And what a stupid bitch I am."

"Don't say that."

Madeleine looked at Maggie.

"We are destined to be friends, I think."

"I hope so."

"No, really. She was taken from us both and now we have each other."

"I'd like that."

"Now. Let me get us each a glass of very cold, very excellent *rosé*, and I will tell you who murdered our dear Brigitte and how stupid the police are not to have even questioned the man yet."

7

G race and Maggie were seated across from each other at *Le Canard*. For the first time in months, they both wore light sweaters. Leaves carpeted the flagstones on the café terrace. The scent of autumn hung in the air.

Maggie was reading from her notebook.

"As simple as rubbing cut garlic on toasted pieces of day-old French bread. As rudimentary, yet essential, as tossing green olives with a little olive oil and hot pasta. Simple, good farmhouse cooking in France remains the keystone to the country's cuisine and culinary pride."

Grace tossed down the fashion magazine she had been flipping through and looked up at Maggie.

"Is that true?" Grace said.

"It doesn't have to be true. I can just put it forward as true, being the author and all."

"But what if someone wants to say that the more complex sauces and stews that France is known for, its wizardry with pastries and such—something no housewife in her right mind would ever attempt—that these are the keystones to the country's cuisine? Hardly simple! I mean, they could make an argument, you know."

"Shut up, Grace."

"Yeah, well, I can do that. The rest of it sounded great, darling. Really cookbookish. I'm serious. Made me hungry."

"Shut up, Grace."

"So what else did Madeleine say? You really think she's had work? She can't be thirty-eight years old. Maybe it was corrective, you know? Fixing a harelip or something?"

Maggie rolled her eyes at her friend and put down her notes. She signaled a waiter to bring them two more coffees.

"I told you most of what she said and I also told you I liked her."

"I'm so pleased for you, angel."

"Look, you're the one who's leaving me," Maggie said. "Let's please not forget who's bugging off to the States and leaving me here barely able to order my own *baguettes* at the market."

"I'm feeling sad, Maggie."

"Oh, again shut up, Grace. You're not sad. You want to go—you're *happy* to go! You just don't like the idea that I might not be so stinking lonely after all when you leave and isn't that an ugly way to feel about your best friend?"

"Oh, how I'm going to miss being made to feel small and mean by you."

"I'm ignoring you."

"So tell me about the investigation. Can you do that? Can we talk about who killed Brigitte without hearing a rundown of all the new best friends you've collected in the meantime?"

"You're doing this to make it easy on me, aren't you, Gracie? That's so sweet of you! Like throwing rocks at Lassie because you know she'll get in trouble for being with you but it just breaks your heart to do it. That is just so effing sweet."

"I expected to be missed, Maggie. Is that so terrible? Yes, I do want to go. Can't it still hurt to leave you? And can't it hurt to think I'm so damn replaceable? What's it been? Two possible best friend replacements in forty-eight hours?"

"No one could ever take your place, Grace."

The two friends were silent for a moment.

"I'm sorry," Grace said. "There's no easy way to leave someone you care about. Maybe I'm trying to make you the bad guy because I can't stand to think I'm doing this deliberately."

Maggie reached over and gripped Grace's hand. The waiter set down new coffees frothy with steamed milk.

"Pijou said she propositioned Bedard, did I tell you?" Maggie dumped a packet of sugar crystals into her coffee.

Grace grinned. "She's such a tart, isn't she? But Bedard *is* awfully cute. He eyes you pretty good, Madame Dernier."

"Don't be absurd."

"Like you don't know it. So did you ring him up and tell him about Madeleine's choice of suspects?"

Maggie shook her head. "Saying Brigitte was having it off with the hospital pharmacist didn't impress me as a good enough reason to believe the guy did it."

"But he could have?"

Maggie shrugged. "I'm going to go talk to him."

"You're not!" Grace smiled broadly. "Boy, this is like old times, isn't it? Want some help? I can knock over some enema kits or something while you rifle his work diary."Maggie ignored her.

"The reason I didn't call Bedard was because I had nothing but gossip to pass on. And since I didn't feel in the mood to be condescended to, I thought I'd wait until I had a confession or something like that."

"God, isn't it weird all the sleeping around this crowd does? I mean Yves does it with everyone, including Madeleine and Pijou, and now Brigitte with this guy? I would've liked to have thought that she was, you know, the injured party, but not if she was screwing around too. "

"I didn't know what to think when Madeleine told me," Maggie admitted. "I mean, it's true we didn't know Brigitte very well, but it was still shocking."

"Do you believe Madeleine?"

"Why would she lie to me? She loved Brigitte. She thought she was passing on the name of Brigitte's killer."

"And what was that name, exactly?"

Maggie flipped open her notebook again.

Grace laughed. "You keep your murder investigation notes all mixed up with your cookbook notes?"

Maggie ignored her question. "His name is Jean-Paul Remey."

"Never heard of him."

"Can't imagine why you would."

"And the police are telling you nothing?"

"Nada. Bedard is true to his word."

"Oh, well, you didn't need his help with Connor," Grace said, referring to the mutual friend who had been murdered at Maggie and Laurent's home two years earlier.

"Sometimes I still can't believe Connor's dead," Maggie said. "He was so much fun and so full of life."

Grace opened her purse to extricate the required euros for the coffees.

"Right!" she said brightly. "What's next? The hospital? Monsieur Pill-Mixer? I suppose we're safe enough there if he should happen to feel cornered and want to elude us by slitting our throats."

"I'm going alone, Grace. Thanks for the offer all the same."

"You can't go alone! Did Nancy Drew go without George? Did Lucy go without Ethel? Did Thelma handle it without Louise? Well, skip that last one."

Maggie laughed.

"Don't you have children sorts of things to do? Where's Zouzou?"

"I have plenty of things to do, Maggie, dearest. I'm moving in two weeks in case you've forgotten. I just thought this would be a good opportunity to spend some time together."

Maggie stood up and tossed down her own coins for the coffees.

"Come to dinner tomorrow night and bring Win and the kids. Laurent said to make sure I reminded you."

"It's hardly as exciting as tracking and belling the killer in his lair."

"Then you've obviously forgotten Laurent's *béchamel* sauce. It doesn't get any more exciting. Maybe I should write that down."

"You'll never convince me, darling."

"Fortunately, I don't have to. I'm sure my editor will think it's all terribly authentic and that's all that matters."

"If you say so." Grace gathered up her Prada handbag and gloves and stood next to Maggie. "Personally, I cannot imagine people getting so excited about putting meals together. What next? The art of dishwashing?"

Maggie looked at Grace with surprise. She knew Grace didn't cook but it had never occurred to her that her friend might not be able to appreciate good food.

"Well, maybe leaving France won't be so devastating for you, after all," she said.

Maggie cut the tomato into thin slices.

Spontaneity and simplicity, she thought as she worked. *Make it quick. Make it close to its natural state. That's the key. No grinding and manipulating of the foods. No heavy seasonings either.*

She tossed chunks of blue cheese into a large earthenware bowl of mesclun and added careful drops of a port vinaigrette.

What was all this to Grace? Just fuel? Just so many nutrients arranged in a tasty manner? Maybe she should go back to the United States.

Maggie put down her knife and stared out the window and found herself wondering when it had changed for herself.

When had she stopped missing *Tijuana Flats* and started to appreciate the artistry and wonder of French cuisine? In her heart, she believed she always had. It wasn't something one had to learn. And besides, Laurent had always loved cooking for her.

She sighed and scanned the horizon for his familiar form. She couldn't see him but she knew he was out there somewhere surrounded by his beloved grapes.

Grace had mentioned over their coffees that she had been to see Marie several times and that her state of mind had not improved. She was still a basket case, unable to take comfort from Grace's visits.

The landline rang in the salon and Maggie wiped her hands on a kitchen towel before answering it.

"*Allo,*" she said. She hated answering the phone when Laurent wasn't here. Understanding French was even trickier when you didn't have the helpful sign language that Maggie depended on for communication.

"Maggie? This is Detective Inspecteur Bedard."

Maggie felt her pulse jump.

"How is the cookbook coming, eh?"

"Fine, thanks."

"Remind me to give you my grandmother's *aïoli* recipe. It is by far the best. It will help you sell many books."

"Oh, good," Maggie laughed. "I only have about a dozen *aïoli* recipes now. I think my next book will be all the variations of *aïoli* in France!"

"*Alors,* Maggie," Bedard continued. "I am calling to say I know about your attempt to talk to Jean-Paul Remey."

"How in the world did you—" she began.

"I'm calling to say that my office has received a complaint from Monsieur Remey about that attempt."

"Are you serious?"

What was this Remey-guy's problem?

Maggie had just left a note saying she'd come by and would like to ask him a few questions.

"When I told him that you were not connected with the investigation, he became very angry."

"Don't you think it's unusual that he reacted like that?" she asked. "Maybe an over-reaction?"

"You cannot ask people questions in connection with this case, Maggie."

"Why not?"

"You are interfering with the official investigation."

Maggie thought she could detect the first signs of exasperation from the typically cool Bedard.

"Had you already questioned Remey?" she asked.

"That is none of your business."

"Is he a suspect?"

"Maggie, I will have to have a word with your husband if you persist in this."

Was this guy for real?

Maggie nearly burst out laughing.

"Well, I'm sorry to disappoint you, Detective, but Laurent doesn't tell me what to do. I'm an *American* wife."

"More's the pity. I will have no more complaints about your intervention in this matter. Do you understand?"

"So next time you'll arrest me?" Maggie's face felt hot.

"Next time I will not speak with you at all," Bedard said. "I will deal with this matter through Monsieur Dernier."

Nearly sputtering with rage, Maggie hung up on the detective.

∿

Grace tucked Zouzou into her car seat, buckled her in and then slid into the driver's seat, careful not to crush her new Donna Karan silk stole.

Really too fussy for a trip to the pediatrician.

But true to who she was, she wore it anyway, and with pleasure.

Zouzou chattered to herself in the backseat, leaving Grace to her thoughts and the scenes of French countryside that seemed to have the color leached from them with every mile.

Ever since her classes with Marie, Grace had found herself more and more attentive to things she'd never bother to notice before.

Clouds, for example. The way they billowed and puffed, their edges stained with violet or dark bruises of color, depending on the impending weather.

Grace was surprised at how much pleasure she'd begun to get simply by watching each day's sky.

At the sign for Aix she turned off the A20. It was just a routine wellness check-up. Win had suggested that it might be better to get it done now in case it got lost in the shuffle once they were Stateside.

Grace's faith in French doctors had taken a serious hit ever since Princess Diana. But French doctors *had* managed to get Grace pregnant two years ago, and she was willing to forgive much for that.

Grace stared at the mildly uncompromising landscape. Autumn had edged into the scenes, with flowering stands of bright red leaves climbing up windowsills and ancient trees, replacing the verdant fields with their own brilliance.

There was so much she missed about America. It wouldn't have done to let on to Maggie. No, that was Maggie's special real estate: being homesick, missing her Southern home. Grace was happy to play the polyglot, the sophisticate who was comfortable in all cultures.

The facts were slightly different, she had to admit. Try as she did to portray herself as something else, the fact was she missed home, she missed the familiarity of her own country, and the relief that comes when everyone you meet is speaking your language.

And then Windsor had handed her the way out. Through no device of her own, she was being allowed to leave and go back home.

It was perfect. She had all the stories to recount of her years of living in France, ("Zouzou was born there, you know") all the soon-to-be-made friends in their wealthy new subdivision in Zionsville—just north of Indianapolis—to be wildly impressed by the pictures of her French mansion in the countryside of the south of France. ("It broke my heart to leave France. Always, it will be home to me.")

She glanced in the rearview mirror at her youngest daughter. With Zouzou's tiny ears pierced with little loops of gold, her exotic name, and her fluent French vocabulary, Grace considered Zouzou to be her great French accomplishment.

Silly, of course. With my and Win's genes she's as American as Sears and Roebuck.

Grace's smile broadened as she gazed at her child. She drove into Aix, deftly cutting in front of another driver and then squeezing her Mercedes into a close parking spot.

Zouzou of course will remember nothing of her experience here. Brought to life on French soil after so much effort and pain and now, never to remember that France was a part of her, except through old photographs.

Grace sat in the parked car with her seat belt still secure around her.

And of course, there was Taylor.

Grace found herself nearly wincing at the thought. Taylor, so nervous and unhappy until she came to France and found her precious Nanny—the one person on earth who could tame and moderate the awful child. Grace felt a flush of guilt for the thought.

How would Taylor react to the kind of stimulation endured by most American children? How would her tortured, brilliant seven-year-old handle America with its violent television and video games, and its continuous untrammeled consumption?

Grace rubbed her eyes with one hand, unmindful of what it would do to her mascara. Zouzou cooed happily in the back seat.

Now that this part of my life has come to an end, Grace thought, the first wash of hopelessness beginning to sift over her, *is the best of my life now behind me?*

Maggie closed her eyes and took a deep breath. The packet of green granules she'd dumped into the bathtub water had read: "Aromatherapy. Guaranteed to relieve stress."

She slipped into the hot water and felt the ministrations overpower her natural copywriter's cynicism. She felt the stress seep out of her pores like sweat. *Finally,* she thought, as she lay back in the bath, *advertising copy that you can believe.*

Thirty minutes later, as she was hoisting her totally relaxed, very limp body out of the now cooled tub water, she heard Laurent's dog bark from the kitchen below.

That's odd. Laurent doesn't allow the dog in the house.

As eager as she was to debrief Laurent on her phone conversation with Bedard, Maggie felt the twinge of anxiety as she pulled on her terrycloth robe and opened the bathroom door.

"Laurent?" she called down the stairs.

There was no answer except the sound of pounding dog feet coming up the stairs to her and then the yipping as Petit-

Four who was curled up on a bath towel on the floor of the bathroom greeted the newcomer.

Oh, great, Maggie thought, closing the bathroom door to keep the big dog from jumping on her. A mixed breed standard poodle, the animal hit into the bathroom door with both feet, making Petit-Four bark again.

Maggie could hear Arlo's labored breathing. She opened the door and put a hand out to him.

"Settle down, boy," she said soothingly. "Where is your papa, eh?"

Within seconds, she heard the downstairs door crash open.

That was not Laurent's style.

"Laurent?"

She pulled the belt of her robe tightly around her and stepped out into the hall. Her fingers felt for the collar of the big dog beside her.

"Ah, *oui*, it is me," he called to her. "You were expecting someone else?"

Was he drunk?

Maggie wrapped her wet hair in a towel and walked downstairs, Petit-Four at her heels. The big dog ran ahead of her.

"Why'd you make so much noise coming in? And why is Arlo in the house?"

As soon as she saw him, Maggie froze.

He stood, nearly belligerently, in front of her. His long hair was tossed by the cold air outside and his cheeks were flushed red. He wore his usual jeans and ancient pullover, his beefy arms stuffed into his trademark corduroy jacket. He glared at her as if in a challenge.

In his right hand, he held the long, wicked stock of a hunting rifle. Arlo bounded over to his master. In his enthusiasm, the dog's tail knocked over a small Lladro sculpture on the coffee table. The figurine broke into two pieces.

"What is that stupid dog doing in here?" she shrieked. "And what do you mean bringing that gun in my home?"

She picked up the broken Lladro and swept the ceramic dust into her hand.

"That dog is not allowed in this house. You are responsible for this."

"I will pay for the silly thing," Laurent said.

She snapped her head up to look at him.

"It was a gift from my parents," she said hotly. "Will you pay to have the sentimentality restored? Or am I to be falling all over myself with gratitude that I'll have a glued-together facsimile in its place?"

"Perhaps you are too sentimental," Laurent said, hoisting the rifle with one hand and nudging the dog out of the door with the heel of his boot.

"What are you doing with that damn gun?"

Maggie felt she could physically attack Laurent at this moment. Her anger made her clutch her fist, the shards of the broken sculpture cutting into her palm.

"I will be hunting this season," Laurent said over his shoulder to her.

"We talked about this."

"We did not come to the conclusion that I would not hunt."

"You know how I feel."

"I know how you feel about a great many things, Maggie," he said, affecting a tiredness in his voice. "How can I avoid knowing so much about your wants? What you don't have? What you need? What you won't put up with, eh?"

"You're a total bastard."

"Perhaps," Laurent said, with a shrug. "But I *will* hunt."

"Hunt then." Maggie jerked her robe tightly around her and planted her feet in front of him. She brought her face close to his seemingly impassive one.

"Hunt until you blow a few toes off. Hunt for food we don't need. Hunt to be a big man with all the other big men."

"I have heard this all before. I'm going to clean up for dinner."

Without a backward glance, he turned and left the house, leaving Maggie fuming with impotent rage.

He deliberately came to provoke me! He came just to let me know he'd decided to shoot and I'd just have to deal with it.

She walked to the French door and watched Laurent as he jerked open the door to the garden shed and placed the rifle inside. She watched him run his hand through his hair and then stand, his hands on his hips, staring contemplatively at the ground, his dog sniffing at the door of the shed.

All at once, it seemed childishly clear to Maggie that Laurent had made his aggressive presentation to her because he wanted the fact that he would be hunting this season out in the open. And as stubborn as he obviously intended to be about it, he clearly did not take her reaction lightly—why else stage this overdrawn confrontation to bring it to a head?

It didn't make her feel much better about the idea of a gun so close to the house but at least he had treated her reaction with respect.

Maggie backed away from the window to avoid being seen as Laurent walked back to the house.

She'd lost this battle about him hunting, she thought, as she watched him approach the house—his face set in a grim mask —but the war?

Perhaps that was another thing.

8

S he died here.

Maggie stood at the edge of the highway and looked into the shallow ditch that cradled the road. Amazingly, after eight days, the spot where Brigitte's body was found was still matted and scarred. It had rained hard only once since then. The day of the funeral.

The ground felt hard and ungiving beneath her sneakered feet. It was late August. Hunting season was approaching. Maggie's thoughts went to Laurent. He was home preparing for the dinner party they would give that evening. The matter of whether he would or wouldn't hunt, unresolved for now.

It was a fine balance of forgiveness and frigidity that had met Laurent on his return from the garden shed. Maggie found a nugget of comfort in his apprehension of her reaction to the guns, yet she felt the need to remind him—in whatever way she could—that she was not happy about the gun.

And so they did not make love last night, but she kissed him good-bye this morning before she left, and she felt him relax some of the tension he'd been holding onto.

Now, as she stood at the site of Brigitte's last terrified moments on earth, she felt bewildered.

Why here? Had she been raped elsewhere and dumped here? If so, had she still been alive when she'd been thrown from the car?

Maggie stepped into the ditch, careful not to step on the matted down spot, like it was a grave. The police had obviously combed the area well. Maggie walked to the far side of the ditch and looked on the other side.

From here she could see the ground sloped gradually down another eight feet to a line of ancient sycamores. They looked sick and spindly and Maggie wondered how much longer the Provençal rain and sparse soil could sustain them. She locked her knees and slid to the bottom of the small hill, leaving Brigitte's site above her.

A series of high cypresses flanked the sycamores and Maggie walked toward them. She thought she could actually smell the Provençal herbs baking in the late summer sun. She stopped, closed her eyes, and took a deep breath to see whether she could pick out the scent of lavender.

Grace will miss the lavender, she thought, feeling the sun caress her face. *She'll miss the constant, relentless beauty of this place too.*

Maggie opened her eyes and smiled.

She'll make up for it with all the exaggerated stories she'll be able to spin.

The smile vanished as Maggie thought of Connor.

And some not so exaggerated.

Turning away from the cypresses, Maggie prepared to hike back up the steep incline when her eye caught something glint in the sunlight. Vaguely mindful of the region's pit vipers that lurked in tall grass, Maggie picked her way to the spot directly below where Brigitte's body had been found.

At first she tried to push the grass away with her foot but

then, ignoring the threat of snakes, reached into the undergrowth and grabbed the shining, gold tube of lipstick.

Clarins, to be exact.

"So does that mean Madeleine killed her?" Grace asked.

Maggie sat in her car in the hospital parking lot and spoke on her cell phone. It was the first time since she left Domaine St-Buvard that she'd gotten any reception at all.

She peered out at the group of hospital personnel scurrying past her in the parking lot.

"I guess a lot of people use Clarins lipstick," Maggie said.

"I have done," Grace said on the other end of the line. "But I didn't kill Brigitte."

"Thanks, Gracie. Always helpful to eliminate the field."

"You going to tell Bedard?"

"Nope."

"Oh, you are naughty, Maggie! Isn't that withholding evidence?"

"Screw him," Maggie said, as she spied Yves walk by. "His men should have done a better job of looking at the murder site. Bunch of incompetents!"

"He's not going to like this."

"Listen, there's Yves. I gotta go. Wish me luck."

"I do, darling, but be careful. You need to be alive to host tonight's party. Laurent would be furious."

"See you tonight! Bye!" Maggie disconnected and stepped out of the car.

"*Excusez-moi*, Yves? Yves Genet?"

Yves was walking with a colleague but stopped and turned to face Maggie. Without looking at his companion, he dismissed him with a wave and gave Maggie his full attention.

Maggie swallowed hard. It occurred to her that she'd never

really talked to Yves alone. It also occurred to her that there was a good possibility he was a murderer.

"Mademoiselle Dernier?" he said, walking toward her.

"*Madame,*" Maggie responded, and found herself blushing.

"Ah, yes, but of course, you are married. How could I forget?"

"I wanted to talk to you about Brigitte."

Yves took Maggie by the arm.

"Let us be alone with this talk," he said.

Maggie allowed him to lead her through a side entrance of the hospital and down a long hall to a small room off the nurse's station. As they walked, she noticed several nurses deliberately averting their eyes as she and Yves passed.

The room Yvea led her to was clearly an examination room. It held a paper-covered examining table. But with stacks of white hospital linens piled up in the corner and on a tall floor-to-ceiling bookshelf, it appeared to be used mostly for storage.

Yves sat down in the sole chair in the room leaving only the table if Maggie chose to sit too. He clasped his hands together and smiled at her. Maggie half expected him to rub his hands together. She felt a pulse of panic in her throat and fought to steady her nerves.

"Now," he said. "What do you have to say about Brigitte?"

Maggie forced herself to smile at him. After all, he would tell her nothing if he didn't want to.

"I was hoping you would tell me the last time you saw her."

Yves raised an eyebrow.

"René believes that the last time I saw his daughter was when I held the knife to her throat."

"Brigitte wasn't killed with a knife."

Yves smiled a little unpleasantly now.

"Just so," he said.

"She was battered to death."

"And I knew this, of course."

"It's not a secret," Maggie said. "If it were, then I wouldn't know it. The police have released this information."

She looked into Yves' eyes, trying to find the thing there that had once made Brigitte love him.

"I don't know what René thinks," Maggie said, consciously trying to put Yves at his ease. "But I haven't heard any evidence to back up the theory that you killed her."

"You are cold-blooded, Madame!" Yves laughed. "People think Americans are so emotional, yes? Such pushovers. But it's not so. I find Americans can see the idea of death so much easier than the rest of us. You are inured, I think. Your American TV makes a little death here and there so much more bearable."

Maggie waited.

"We met here that day in this very room," he said, waving his arm toward the examining table. "We screwed. And intended to meet later that evening for dinner with friends."

Maggie felt her stomach heave. She could not get around the idea of Brigitte loving this man.

"What friends?"

"Madeleine and Richard," Yves said, looking at his watch.

"But you didn't meet them."

"No, Brigitte died instead."

"When did you realize the evening would not happen?"

"The three of us met at the restaurant. Brigitte never showed up."

"Did you eat anyway?"

Yves shrugged. "Why not?

"What restaurant?"

Yves grinned at her. "What a funny little thing you are. *L'Aubergine.*"

L'Aubergine was Uncle August's restaurant.

"One last question," Maggie said. "I know you're busy."

She dug into her handbag.

"Not too busy, really, for a quick one, as you Americans say." Yves said, patting the examining table. "Brigitte, I'm sure, would not mind."

Maggie pulled out the Clarins lipstick.

"Would you know if this was Brigitte's?"

"It is not. Are we finished?" Yves opened the door and strode out.

"Are you sure about the lipstick?" Maggie called after him. She watched as four nurse's faces looked up abruptly from the front desk as she emerged from the room.

"Brigitte never wore make-up," Yves said over his shoulder. "She didn't need it."

Do the police know Brigitte was to have dined at her Uncle August's restaurant. Had August Moreau been questioned?

Yves had been straightforward with Maggie. He probably had been the same with the cops. On the other hand, the cops had missed a lot. Maybe they didn't know about the date at *L'Aubergine*.

Or in the examination room earlier that day.

Maggie stepped into the elevator and pushed the button for the main floor. Her mind whirled with what Yves had told her.

The elevator doors opened and Maggie stepped out. Straight ahead of her was the hospital pharmacy. And there, standing hunched over a tray of rolling pink pills, was a balding man with a white jacket on. Maggie marched into the pharmacy and over to where the man stood at the pharmacist's desk. She read his name badge from the doorway.

"Dr. Remey?" Maggie asked politely. "I am Maggie Dernier. I came here yesterday to ask you a few questions about Brigitte Genet."

Jean-Paul lifted his tragically pocked face to Maggie and rearranged his unfortunate features into an angry grimace.

"Get out of here," he growled. "Or I will have hospital security throw you out!"

"Your English is very good," Maggie said, nonplussed. After all, they were in a public setting. "I just wanted to ask you one question about your relationship with Madame Genet."

"Get out!" Jean-Paul shrieked. He pounded his fist on the counter in front of him. The little pink pills jumped in their plastic dish.

Maggie noticed a couple people back out of the drugstore and scurry away. She felt a vein of annoyance. What was this guy hiding? He clearly had a temper and while he probably wasn't going to tell her anything deliberately, it occurred to her that he just might let something slip in a temper.

"Look," she said sweetly. "I don't know why you're getting so upset. I just want to know if you were sleeping with Brigitte, okay?"

Without warning, the man vaulted over the counter and pushed Maggie into one of the store aisles, screaming in incomprehensible French, spittle forming in foamy pockets in the corners of his mouth.

Maggie rolled away from him, knocking over a magazine display carousel that caught the enraged pharmacist across the brow.

She grabbed a wooden crutch that had clattered to the floor beside her but Jean-Paul wrenched it from her hands and grabbed her by the shoulders and shook her violently, screaming like a madman.

Helpless to stop him, Maggie flailed impotently with her hands. Maggie knew she was about to black out when she was suddenly dropped to the floor.

Her skull hummed in pain, her vision cloudy, as she lay on the floor panting and listening to the cacophony of people talking and yelling around her. Over the din she heard a siren begin to wail and more people seemed to crowd into the small drugstore.

A man knelt beside her and gently touched her face. Maggie's eyes focused slowly.

"Are you all right, Madame?" the voice said. The man touched her neck and probed her head. "Can you see me, Madame Dernier? Open your eyes."

It was Madeleine's husband, Richard. His face was close to hers, his eyes looking worriedly into hers.

"I see you," Maggie said in a whisper.

"*Dieu merci*," he said softly.

He pulled her to a sitting position. Within seconds he placed a bottle of water in her hands

"Drink a little."

"Where is Jean-Paul?"

Richard made a sound of disgust.

"The man belongs in an asylum. He's been taken away."

"*Mon dieu!* What has happened?" Yves said. He knelt down next to Maggie. "You should have told me you wanted to talk to Jean-Paul, Madame Dernier. I could have saved you the concussion. The man's a lunatic. What happened?"

Richard spoke quickly to Yves in French. Finally, Yves whistled, then laughed.

"I wish I could have seen that!" he said. "You pulling Remey off Madame Dernier and punching him in the nose! Incredible!"

Maggie looked up at Richard. "You punched him in the nose?"

"He's being lucky I did not grind his head with his own pestle!"

The three of them laughed. Then Maggie allowed herself to be helped to her feet. For a moment, when reflected in Richard's simple charity and grace, she had gotten a strong if brief feeling for why Brigitte may have been able to tolerate Yves. Richard brought out the human element in Yves. And she could see how that could be nice.

"I don't know how I can thank you," she said to Richard. "I had no idea he was unstable."

"Il n'y a pas de quoi," Richard said, dusting off his slacks. "It gives me a little something to brag about to Madeleine, eh?"

"Have her call me," Maggie said. "I'll brag plenty about you."

Richard looked up at Yves. "Is the alert from the Emergency Room?"

Before Yves could answer a young nurse rushed into the pharmacy.

"Dr. Genet!" she said breathlessly. "It's your sister-in-law, Pijou Pernon. In the Emergency Room."

9

L aurent ladled the *bourride* onto the fish fillet and handed the bowl to Maggie.

"Parsley would be good," he said.

Ignoring his suggestion, Maggie took the bowl and walked it to the dining room table where she placed it with the others on the table.

"Need one more," she called into the kitchen.

"So, tell me," Grace said, putting down her glass of California Chardonnay as she got up from the sofa. Her tunic fell in silken folds around her slim frame. "How much does Laurent know of yesterday?"

Maggie touched the bruise above her right eye. "He thinks I walked into a wall."

"Brilliant."

"He knows I talked with Yves."

"How'd he take that?"

Maggie shrugged and smiled as Laurent entered the dining room with the last bowl of *bourride.*

"We are ready, yes?" he said, not answering Maggie's smile with his own.

"I think so," Maggie said. "Windsor? You want to bring the kiddies to the table?"

"Not really," Windsor said, getting to his feet. "Where's that babysitter?"

"Now, now," Grace said as she scooped up little Zouzou and put her in her high chair. "Why would you need a babysitter at a dinner party?"

"Why indeed?" Windsor said, smiling at Maggie. He looked tired. "Where do we sit?"

They took their places and Laurent handed a warm piece of bread to Taylor. He spoke softly in French.

"I love *bourride!*" Grace said, seating herself at the table. "As only you can make it, darling Laurent. So," she continued, this time looking at Maggie. "What is the story about Pijou?"

"Still alive. And according to Yves likely to remain so."

"You mean he saved her?" Windsor said.

"More like he diagnosed her," Maggie said. "She *was* seriously hurt."

"So Pijou, she is fine?" Laurent asked..

"Well, no," Maggie said slowly. "She's in a coma."

"And you can't tell us how she came to be that way because of the ildren-chay, right?" Grace said.

"And she cannot talk over their heads in a foreign language," Laurent said, "because she doesn't know any."

Grace and Windsor exchanged a look. *Uh-oh.*

"Taylor and the baby both understand French," Maggie said.

"Which is more than can be said of you, *chérie*," Laurent said.

"Did I mention how much I love this *bourride*?" Grace said brightly.

"I understand French. Lots of it," Maggie said.

"Tu es magnifique."

"Et tu es un jerk.*"*

"Come on, you guys," Grace said, putting a hand on Maggie's hand.

Laurent pushed back his chair and lit up a cigarette.

"Did she tell you how she got the bruise on her head?"

"Laurent, the children," Maggie said. "Don't smoke at the—"

"Because I personally have not yet heard how. Have I, Maggie? Not the truth."

"This is ridiculous," Maggie said, looking uncomfortably at their dinner guests.

"She talks to Genet—a major suspect in a murder investigation—" Laurent said.

"He's not a major suspect," Maggie interrupted.

"How do you know that? Is your good friend Bedard telling you he is not? Or is this Maggie being smarter than everyone else?"

"I can't believe you're going to ruin this dinner," she said.

"I made this dinner, how can I ruin it?"

"That must be French logic. It's lost on me."

"As are most things French, yes, *chérie*?"

The knock on the door caused everyone to jump.

"Oh, my God, I think I swallowed an olive pit," Grace said, coughing.

Windsor gave Grace a couple of gentle slaps on the back and Zouzou knocked over her milk.

"I'll get it," Maggie said, jumping up and desperate to escape the tension of the table and Laurent's palpable anger at her.

Bedard stood on the door step.

"I know why you're here," Maggie said, her shoulders sagging in defeat. "Bad news travels fast."

"I'm not sure you do know, " Bedard said. He wore jeans and a blue cotton sweater. He was obviously off duty.

Maggie couldn't help but notice that blue did wonderful things for his eyes.

"Did Doctor Reméy put out a warrant for my arrest? Are you here to discuss it with my husband? Because, go ahead. Knock yourself out—it'll be the cherry on his cake, I can tell you."

Bedard ran a hand through his hair and looked back at his car parked in the driveway. He returned his gaze to Maggie.

"You've got to stop driving me crazy," he said in a low voice.

"Who is it, Maggie?" Laurent's voice carried down the hall and out onto the front steps.

"Be there in a minute," she called before turning back to Bedard. "Come inside and we can talk."

Bedard shook his head.

"*C'est très simple.* There is something between us, yes? You are feeling it? I am right, *non?*"

Maggie felt her stomach muscles tighten.

"I am thinking of you too much," Bedard said. "I get a call from the hospital saying Jean-Paul Remey has attacked you and I want to—what do you think?"

Maggie cleared her throat.

"I don't know. What?"

"Well, let me say, I am happy to have to come and see you again. But not to scold you, eh? Maybe to take you into my arms? You are driving me crazy," he said, shaking his head again.

"You're not here tonight officially?"

Bedard gave her an incredulous look. "No," he said. "Not officially."

Maggie closed the door behind her and stepped out onto the porch.

"Look, the whole reason I started asking questions was because I wanted to help," Maggie said. "I still want to help. But partially, maybe, I don't know, maybe I wanted to work with you."

When she saw his face light up, she realized what she'd said. What she had not meant to say.

"Forget I put it like that," she said hurriedly. "I don't know what I'm doing these days.

I was going to call you before things went all crazy with Reméy to tell you I found a tube of Clarins lipstick at the murder site yesterday morning."

"What?"

"Yves said it's not Brigitte's but it's not all rusty and nasty either so it hadn't been there long. So, unless you employ cross-dressers, my guess is the killer may have dropped it."

Bedard stared at her and his mouth fell open.

"Your men missed it, Roger," Maggie said.

"*Sacre bleu!*"

Bedard looked like he didn't know which statement aston-ished him more. That his men had missed an important piece of evidence or that Maggie had talked to the victim's husband.

"You talked to Genet?"

"Today at the hospital."

Bedard turned and looked again in the direction of his car.

"I'll need the lipstick," he said wearily.

"Of course."

"Look, I have an idea."

Bedard ran his hand through his short brown hair again. Maggie recognized it this time as a familiar gesture. She had seen Laurent do it many times during times of stress and agitation.

"I will give you some of the information you have been asking for," he said. "In exchange, you will inform me of who you are to speak to and when."

"I can't do that," Maggie said hurriedly, aware that she had been gone from her dinner party for a long time. "Sometimes I don't know myself until it happens. The Jean-Paul thing was totally unplanned. I just saw him and went for it."

"And then he went for you."

Bedard touched the bruise on her forehead with an index finger.

Maggie pulled away.

"Besides, if I tell *you* then you'll warn me not to do whatever it is I was about to do."

"Or I could accompany you."

"You'd come with me?"

"I don't know. Maybe."

He looked into her face and Maggie had the terrifying feeling he was about to kiss her.

"You must stop talking to people who may be violent—who may be killers."

Maggie saw a shadowed movement in Bedard's car. He turned to look at his car too.

"There wasn't a better time to come," he said. "And I couldn't get a sitter without any notice."

"That's your daughter?"

"She was sleeping when I arrived. Wait here." He walked back to the car. Maggie watched him open the back door. Within a few seconds, he returned.

"She's still asleep," he said.

"How in the world do you do your job with a child?"

"I wouldn't have brought her if I thought there was going to be trouble," Bedard said wryly.

"You're welcome to leave her with me sometime."

"That is an incredible offer, Madame."

Maggie shrugged. "I like kids."

The front door suddenly opened.

"Inspector," Laurent said, nodding at Bedard. "*Y a-t-il un problème?*"

Bedard looked at Maggie and shook his head.

"I think we've solved it," he said.

"Then, come in. Have a drink." Laurent nodded toward the car. "Bring your friend."

He's got the eyesight of a Great Horned Owl.

"She's underage," Bedard said smoothly. "And it is late. Madame Dernier, I will discuss this further with you tomorrow, yes? Monsieur, *merci pour tout et bonne nuit.*" He turned abruptly, got in his car, and drove away.

Maggie and Laurent both watched Bedard's brake lights disappear into the dark night.

"Back to the party, *chérie*?" Laurent asked gently.

The candles still flickered on the dining room table. An hour after Maggie's doorstep conversation with Bedard, Taylor had been sidetracked by some imagined insult by her baby sister and disintegrated into a full-blown tantrum.

She was carried screaming out of the Dernier house by her weary father.

Grace lingered a moment in the doorway with the sleeping Zouzou in her arms. Her face suddenly looking lined and old to Maggie.

"In spite of everything," Grace said, "It was a good evening."

"It was a shambles," Maggie said, touching the baby's cheek with the tips of her fingers. "Mostly my fault."

Grace smiled weakly. "The first year is always the toughest."

"Yeah, I know," Maggie said, kissing her friend on the cheek. "Charles Boyer and *Gaslight.*"

"Call me," Grace said as Windsor walked back up the front steps to take Zouzou from her.

Maggie watched the car disappear into the gloom. She saw no flailing arms in the back seat and guessed that Taylor had found at least temporary peace in sleep.

"Even the rich have their troubles," Laurent said, coming up behind her. He placed his hands on her shoulders and she relaxed into them. "I'm sorry for tonight."

"Me, too," Maggie said.

He turned her around to face him and they kissed.

"I don't know why I have said these things," he said.

"Let's forget it," she said. "It's been a long night and the unpleasantness isn't totally your or my fault." She closed the front door and followed him into the kitchen.

"We can do it in the morning," he said, gesturing to the piles of pots and pans in the sink.

"Let's at least get a jump on it," Maggie said picking up a thickly encrusted casserole.

They worked in silence, the only noise the hum of the water from the tap and the sounds of china and crystal clinking musically together.

"What did you think of Marie?" Maggie asked, breaking the silence between them.

"Marie? Brigitte's mother? I thought nothing. She is an *artiste*. She wears black. She has a self-concept. I thought nothing."

"Yeah, she does have a self-concept, doesn't she?" Maggie found an assortment of conflicting thoughts crisscrossing her brain. "I wouldn't have expected her to go to pieces like she has."

"She is a mother. It is a terrible loss."

"Yes, of course. I just would've thought she had more steel in her."

"*Artistes* are passionate. They are emotional beings." Laurent threw down a dish towel. "Done for now," he said.

"Yeah, okay," Maggie said. She bent down to push a large Le Creuset pot into the bottom cupboard. "There's something wedged in here," she said, peering into the cupboard.

"Ah, never mind that," Laurent said. "I will put it away."

Maggie drew her hand out of the cupboard, bringing with it a small black handgun that had kept the pot from fitting in its slot.

"*Ach, mon Dieu!*" Laurent swore.

"What in hell is this?" Maggie asked, holding the gun upside down by its stumpy handle. She felt her insides quiver with building fury.

"You are never in this kitchen," Laurent said. "I cannot believe you found it."

"Why is it here?" Maggie handed the gun to Laurent. Her face was crimson.

"I've had it for years."

"A handgun's only purpose is to kill another human."

"Who are you quoting now? Your father?"

"Do not dare to get sarcastic with me, Laurent Dernier! Don't even dream of it! Do you still have enemies? Do we need protection from something you haven't told me about? Is that why you have it?"

"I keep it for sentimental reasons."

"Get rid of it."

Laurent said nothing.

"Look, Laurent, I've given in on the hunting rifle. But I will never give in on the idea of a handgun in my house." She paused for dramatic effect. "And you expect me to someday bring *children* into this house?"

Finally, Laurent nodded. "I'll get rid of it."

"How?"

"It's not registered. I can hardly just hand it in to your friend Detective Inspector Bedard! I will have to throw it into the Rhone. What difference does it make?"

"Just make sure it doesn't resurface in my house."

Laurent wrapped the gun up, the only sound between them the harsh crackle of the paper.

"Promise me on our love that you'll get rid of it."

He looked at her as if startled. Then, "I said I would do it," he said firmly.

The ringing phone woke Maggie at a little before six.

"*Mon Dieu!* Who calls so early?" growled Laurent, rolling over in bed and pressing a pillow over his head.

Maggie sat up in bed and picked up the hand set on her bedside table.

"Hello?" she said.

"Maggie? Is that you? This is Marie Pernon. Oh, Maggie, I must speak to you. Please say you will help me!"

"Marie? Are you okay?"

"Oh, Maggie, you must help me. The police have come this morning—just like the Gestapo—and taken René away! They have arrested my poor René for the killing of our girl!"

"Okay, Marie, calm down." Maggie looked at Laurent who was sitting up in bed now watching her.

"What happened?" he asked.

"It's Marie. The cops arrested René. Please get me some coffee. I'll be down in a minute. Marie? Tell me from the beginning. I cannot believe Bedard would do this!"

"All the police are liars! Please, Maggie, you will help? Grace said you could. My poor Pijou! She may never awaken! My Brigitte is gone from me and now René! Please help me!"

"I will, Marie."

Maggie climbed out of bed and began looking for her clothes from the chair in her room. She felt anger bubbling in her chest.

How could Bedard come here and talk about working with me when he already had a suspect?

"The police are fools!" Marie said. "They think they are finished with this case but now the murderer goes free! You can find him, Madame Dernier. Grace said you could find him!"

"Marie, of course, I will try."

"I have a message from the *monstre,*" Marie said, her voice rising into hysterics. "He has come to me in a dream, his face darkened to mask his identity. He has come to me to gloat over the murders of my children and to boast of the murder yet to be."

Maggie rubbed her eyes.

What is she talking about?

"He came to me," Marie said ominously. "And told me he will kill Grace next."

10

After making arrangements to meet with Marie, Maggie dressed hurriedly and ran downstairs. Laurent was just pouring the coffee.

"René's been arrested," Maggie said. "And Marie asked me to find the real killer."

Laurent looked at her blankly. "And that would be, why?"

"Grace told her about how I helped find out who really killed Connor, I guess."

"I am guessing, too, that Grace did not mention the part where you and she nearly *died* in the course of solving Connor's murder?"

"We didn't die, obviously."

"*Incroyable!* That you are going to go off trying to find killers and murderers—"

"You told me you didn't care if I investigated this."

"I've changed my mind."

"Tough."

"What is *tough*?"

"It is too late to change your mind. I need to help Marie and René."

"You don't know these people!"

"I *do* know them. I knew *her*! Don't you see? Brigitte mattered to me, Laurent. I didn't know her for very long, but we *connected*. I need to do this."

Laurent looked at her, then sighed. He added cream to her coffee.

"I can't handle full cream, Laurent. I have to keep my calorie count under a thousand per cup or I'll be wearing circus tents by Thanksgiving."

"I don't care how fat you get."

Maggie smiled at him.

"I know you don't. But I care." She leaned over and kissed him. "I'm meeting Marie at *Le Canard* so I have to go." She looked guiltily at the remaining dishes from last night's dinner.

"Go on," he said. "Go."

Maggie picked up her cell phone as she drove and dialed the private office number that Bedard had given her. She was mildly aware of not wanting to talk with him where Laurent could overhear. The Detective picked up immediately.

"*Allo.*"

His voice was warm and already familiar to Maggie. Even in her present irritation with him, she could feel the tingling sensation of excitement in her chest at hearing his voice.

"Are you nuts? Arresting René Pernon?"

"Ah, Maggie."

"I cannot *even* believe you."

"I had nothing to do with it. I was taken off the case two days ago."

"Is that why you came by last night? To see how you could get back *on* the case?"

"You know why I came by last night."

Silence.

Maggie turned into the parking lot of *Le Canard* and immediately spotted Marie sitting at a table on the terrace.

"Look, now what?" she said into the phone. "Are we going to work together on this?"

"We are."

"And you'll start by filling me in on everything? The autopsy results? The murder weapon? Everything your men found?"

"If it ever gets out I told you, I'll be directing traffic in Nîmes."

"When do we meet?"

Maggie sat close to Marie and held both her hands in her own. Their coffee cups were on the table between them.

Marie looked terrible. Her eyes were red from days of weeping. Her disheveled hair seemed more gray than black and her clothes looked like she had not changed for days. Yet Maggie detected a strength or resolve in Marie that she hadn't seen at the funeral or since Brigitte's death. The steel she had expected to see in the Frenchwoman was there, after all. It was buried deep, but it was there.

"Okay, first tell me how Pijou is," Maggie said.

"She is still unconscious," Marie said, taking a deep breath. "She cannot tell us what happened. She cannot tell us who did it."

"What do the police think happened?"

Marie grimaced. "The police! They say only that she was attacked with a blunt instrument."

Maggie waited.

"She was found beaten in her apartment."

"Who found her?"

Marie shut her eyes tightly.

"René. He went to check on her. She had missed supper. She was not answering her phone."

"Are the police using the fact that René discovered her as evidence against him in some way?"

"Who knows? They are idiots." Marie waved away the approaching waiter without looking at him. Maggie couldn't help but notice how imperious Marie could be.

"And the prognosis? When do they expect Pijou to awaken?"

A flash of pain swept across Marie's face but she did not reply.

"Look, Marie," Maggie said, squeezing her hands. "I know I can help you, okay? But I can't do much with this dream thing. I'm sorry. You dreamt the killer came to you? I mean, if you have a theory about who you think killed Brigitte, please tell me. Let's piece some things together and see what kind of picture we get, you know? Hunch, yes; dream, no. Do you understand?"

Marie smiled sadly at Maggie.

"You Americans are not very mystical, are you?" she said. "Perhaps, yes, we should call it a hunch then. Not a dream. I had a terrible hunch. And his face is disguised in my hunch. But he is known to me, this killer. Of that I am positive."

Using a clean dishtowel, the burly chef wiped the grease from his broad forehead.

Why did the fool have to mention that they'd dined at my restaurant? I'd not even been interviewed by the police up to now. Surely, this new information would interest them.

"Don't be ridiculous," Yves had said on the phone in that self-confident way of his. "No one will listen to the American. Besides, they have arrested my father-in-law. They will not be asking any more questions."

René! Arrested!

August Moreau shook his head.

Poor René!

There would have to be many, many Hail Mary's said to assuage the culpability of this new crime, many hours at Mass spent trying to blot out the deed—or at least the too vivid memory of the deed. And perhaps absolution would never come. August knew that was a real possibility.

Oh, how well he knew that real possibility.

"You're not going to like my questions."

"I'm ready to hear them." Marie sipped her cold coffee and made a face. "Where is that imbecile waiter? He's ignored us all morning."

"I'm wondering about Monsieur Moreau."

"Uncle August?"

"I can't help but think he's involved somehow."

Marie studied Maggie. "Why do you think so?"

"It was at his restaurant Brigitte was to have dined that last night."

Marie frowned.

"But he wasn't there that night," Maggie continued. "I called and asked his head chef. August never showed up."

"What are you trying to say?"

"August had opportunity. I saw him and Brigitte together once and it was obvious he was in love with her."

"That is perverse!"

"Nonetheless, it was my observation."

"You don't know him or you couldn't suggest such a thing. I'm losing faith in you, Maggie."

"He doesn't have to be the *murderer*, Marie. He just has to know something. That's all I'm saying."

Marie tossed down a ten euro note and stood up abruptly. She straightened her dark cardigan down over her hips.

"*Bon.* Let's go talk to him."

Within the hour they were seated in the back room of August Moreau's cozy trendy bistro.

Maggie's stomach growled as the tantalizing scents of *cassoulet* and *pot au feu* drifted from behind the curtain that separated them from the rest of the restaurant.

"I am so sorry to hear about René, *chère* Marie." August shook his massive head and patted Marie's hand. "If I can do anything to help you until he is released, you must let me help you."

He turned to Maggie and nodded solicitously at her.

"You will eat something?" he asked, his face round and red. "Some onion soup perhaps?"

Maggie shook her head but Moreau turned and ordered a staff member to bring her a bowl of soup.

Marie leaned across the table and took the fat man's hand.

"Thank you, August. I have confidence that René will be home soon." She paused briefly. "We have come to talk about Brigitte."

Maggie did not have to look too closely to see the man's pained reaction. He looked anxiously from Marie to Maggie and back again. He cleared his throat but said nothing.

"I have some questions," Marie continued. "And I want direct answers. No bullshit, August!"

"What are you saying to me, Marie? I only tell the truth. Why would I not? I loved Brigitte!"

"Too much, maybe, eh?" Marie said, her eyes bright with challenge.

"What are you saying to me?" August looked horrified, but

Maggie couldn't tell whether his reaction was to the idea or to the fact that the truth had been discovered.

"She was my niece. My brother's daughter! Are you suggesting something sick? Something unclean? Has grief demented you, Marie?"

Maggie was silent and watched the pair.

"You grieve her as I do, I know that, August," Marie said. "I don't think you loved her in an unhealthy way."

"I should hope not."

"But you know something about how she died, of that I am now certain, and you will tell me."

Maggie could hear laughter from the main dining room along with the musical clink of silverware against china.

The tension snapped neatly with the arrival of a waiter who set a large bowl of steaming soup in front of Maggie and placed a spoon beside it. He left without speaking.

August groaned.

"I don't know how it is you know," he said, his voice heavy with remorse. "I told Yves there would be trouble. I told him it was madness."

"*What* was madness?" Maggie said.

August stood and walked to the curtain. He glanced out at the busy dining room and then returned to their private table. He looked as if the walk had aged him ten years.

"I did love her."

"I know you did, " Marie said.

"You do not understand," he said, his eyes filling with tears. "I adored her. How could I not? She was perfection, my Brigitte, my perfect angel."

Marie stared at him in disbelief. "You are a bastard."

He nodded unperturbed. "I know," he said without looking at her. "There is nothing you can tell me about myself that I have not said to myself—in much harsher terms."

Maggie cleared her throat.

"What was the madness that Yves suggested?"

August looked at her as if she had just materialized at the table. He seemed surprised to see her sitting there with a bowl of soup in front of her.

"He arranged for me to, " he said as he covered his face with his hands. "Brigitte, my darling girl, forgive me! *Mon Dieu*, have I aided in your murder? Will I ever know if I have helped kill you?"

"Yves arranged for you to do what?" Marie asked.

"To meet secretly with Brigitte that night," he said, beginning to weep. "He said she wanted to see me and that he was surprised but that she must have been secretly attracted to me all these years and that she had suggested we finally..."

He jerked his face up. The tears had made greasy inroads down his plump cheeks.

"She never showed. Yves set it up so I would not have an alibi for the time of her death. The bastard set it all up for me to take the blame. "

"So even Yves could see your unnatural lust for your own niece," Marie stated flatly.

"It wasn't unnatural," August boomed. "Call it what you must, but you know in your heart that it wasn't incest."

Maggie shook her head.

"I don't know, Monsieur Moreau," she said. "Maybe it's a cultural thing, although I doubt it. In America, the relationship between uncle and niece is very close and any sexual or romantic interaction between them would definitely be considered incest. "

"She wasn't my niece. Tell her, Marie. I may be a stupid old fool but I'm not a pervert. Tell her!."

Maggie looked at Marie with confusion.

"The fat bastard is correct," Marie said. "Brigitte and and Pijou are not his nieces because they are not René's daughters."

11

"Not his daughters? Are you serious?"

Grace shifted the phone to her other ear and spooned more strained beets into Zouzou's willing mouth.

"Not *only* not his real daughters," Maggie said from her seat at an outdoor café table, "but the product of a rape a year before Marie met René."

"Marie was raped? Oh, my God. Well, that might explain a few things about Pijou."

"Let's be kind, Gracie."

"Yeah, yeah, sorry. How awful. So does, like, the whole world know about this except Brigitte and Pijou?"

"Pretty much."

"Not a very modern way of handling things."

"We're not talking a question of biological parenthood, here," Maggie said. "It's one thing to be told you were adopted and quite another to be informed you were the result of an act of violence."

"You're right, of course."

Grace put down the jar of beets and scooped her daughter up into her arms and held her tightly.

"Poor Marie. I can't believe how much misery one person is expected to endure in a lifetime."

"I know. She's an incredible woman. Absolutely remarkable. We split up so she could go visit René in jail. I mean, the interview with Uncle August had to have practically killed her, but she's more sure than ever that we're going to find Brigitte's killer."

"She trusts you. She's smart."

"Grace, did Marie tell you about her dream?"

"The one where I'm next on the list?"

"Yeah, okay, well, just keep your eyes open, okay? Be extra careful."

"You don't really think this lunatic is going to come after me next?"

"Just be mindful."

"I always am, darling. *You* be mindful of your own self. I'm not the one being attacked by crazy French pharmacists. What's the deal with him by the way?"

"I'm supposed to meet with Bedard in a few minutes and he'll let me know why he went so loony and if they're going to keep him locked up."

"You're meeting with Bedard?"

"Is there an echo on this line?"

"Is that wise?"

"In what sense are you wondering if it is wise?"

"Don't be a smart ass, Maggie. You know in what sense I'm talking about. His attraction for you is out in the open now. This is a very dangerous situation for a newly married, mildly discontented expatriate to find herself in. Are you sure you know what you're doing?"

Maggie sighed. "I am not going to betray Laurent or my wedding vows, Grace, if that's what you're asking."

"Oh, no, well, maybe not *intentionally*..."

"Nor am I going to *un*intentionally find myself being seduced."

"Can you honestly say you're not attracted to him, too? Or that things aren't just wobbly enough between you and Laurent right now where you might be a shade, shall we say, receptive?"

"You've definitely got to find something besides babies to occupy your mind, Grace. You're starting to invent soap operas in your head."

"Just so long as you keep yours, darling."

"Look, there he is, I'll ring you later, okay?"

Maggie disconnected and stood up. Bedard had parked his unmarked police cruiser in front of the café. She walked to the car and hopped into the passenger seat.

"*Bonjour*, Roger," she said. She was still a little self-conscious from her conversation with Grace.

"*Salut*, Maggie," Bedard said, grinning at her.

He looks altogether too handsome, Maggie thought.

His brown hair was tossed boyishly around his face and his blue-grey eyes twinkled with pleasure at seeing her.

"Have you got much for me?" Maggie asked and then immediately regretted using this particular American idiom. "I've got some new information for you," she added hastily.

Bedard put the car into gear and pulled away from the curb.

"Then perhaps you should go first."

Maggie gave herself a moment to collect her thoughts. She tried to ignore the feeling of heat generated by sitting so closely to Bedard and the agitation that it caused in her stomach.

"Your men never interviewed August Moreau, did they?"

Bedard frowned. "*Non.*"

"Okay, well, it seems Moreau was lured away to a rendezvous with Brigitte on the night of her murder."

"Lured by whom?"

"Yves Genet.

"For what purpose?"

"Moreau says it was to criminally implicate him in her murder and to put him more firmly in Genet's power."

"For what purpose?"

Maggie shrugged. "Maybe he has some dirt on Yves and this was a way for Yves to control him."

"Dirt?"

"Maybe Yves isn't as clean as he appears looks in this murder case."

"He has an airtight alibi."

"I know. But why else set up Uncle August on the night Brigitte was murdered?"

"Moreau says Madame Genet never appeared?"

"That's right. He says he showed up at the park where Yves told him to meet Brigitte and he waited two hours past the agreed-upon time. Finally, he left and went home."

"Don't you think that sounds strange?"

"In France?"

"Don't be offensive." But Bedard's lips twitched into a smile.

"And it was a park, not a café where people might have seen Moreau and given him an alibi for the time. Nobody saw him. When did you determine that Brigitte was killed?"

"Ten in the evening or thereabouts."

"And Moreau was to have met her at eight. So, yeah, he could have met with her, killed her and disposed of her. The timing puts him right in the murder window."

"What about motive?"

"He was in love with her."

"Ah."

Bedard pulled off the highway onto a remote road leading to an even more remote copse of trees. Maggie began to feel a little uneasy.

"Still worried you'll be seen giving me classified information?" she asked.

"Do I make you nervous?"

When Maggie didn't answer, he added, "Precautions are always advisable." He turned the car's engine off.

"I have to be back in an hour," she said.

"No problem." He turned to face her in the car seat. "So he had motive and opportunity but you don't think Moreau killed her."

Maggie unsnapped her seatbelt and got out of the car. Bedard followed her. The leaves on the vines in the nearby vineyard were orange and brown. The rows of gnarly stalks stretched into the distance. Maggie could see the grapes had already been harvested. She wondered when Laurent would do their vineyard.

"No, I don't," she said. "I think Yves knew he would never meet his wife that night at the restaurant. I think he knew he'd never see her alive again. I think his sending Moreau off to meet her is tied into Yves' intention to kill her."

"You think Yves killed his wife? In spite of his alibi?"

Bedard came around and leaned against the hood near her.

"I think I do," she said. "I don't know how he managed it but he was the one moving the pieces around on the board. That means he's the one who knew what was happening that night. But there's a lot of questions not answered and since you haven't told me what you know, maybe I shouldn't commit just yet."

Bedard shrugged. "The crazy pharmacist first," he said.

"Okay, yeah, what's his deal?"

"He was not in love with Brigitte."

"Could've fooled me."

"He loved her in a different way. Less passionately but perhaps as purely."

"God, you French drive me crazy! Was he having it on with her or not?"

"Monsieur Remey is homosexual. Absolutely devoted to Madame Genet in the most platonic terms."

"Jean-Paul is *gay?*"

"So he insists."

"So why did he become unglued when I asked him a few questions?"

Bedard brought his face inches from hers.

"You were asking him whether he had had a sexual affair with his Madonna. In his eyes, you were insulting his one and only idea of pure womanhood. It's actually quite amusing."

"Only a Frenchman would think so." Maggie said. "So where is he now?"

"You weren't thinking of pressing charges, were you?"

"Not unless you think he's dangerous."

"I don't."

"So, what else? Come on. Give me the details that only you, me and the murderer could possibly know."

"Madame Genet was killed around twenty-two hundred hours. She was beaten to death with a club of some kind. We haven't found the weapon, and we don't have much hope of finding it. She had forced sexual relations an hour before but there was no semen except her husband's."

"Well, isn't that indicting?"

"Maggie, Genet himself told you he had had sex with his wife that afternoon."

"Maybe to cover himself for later on." Maggie gnawed on a fingernail in contemplation. "Anything else?"

"The body was found with a large X marked across her face."

"He *wrote* on her? Bizarre."

Bedard frowned as if trying to make up his mind about something.

"They all did," he said. "The nurse, Catherine, who was

killed the week before and Pijou too. It's clear we're dealing with a serial killer."

Maggie felt a shiver shoot through her.

A serial killer. Did that mean it was less likely to be Yves? Or more?

"An X across the face means a cross out, right?" she said.

"Possibly. Except one would have thought that the murder itself was the ultimate cross out."

"How was the nurse killed?"

"Bludgeoned."

"Raped, too?"

Bedard nodded.

"All three victims are connected in some way to Yves' hospital," Maggie said.

"I'm surprised to hear you rule out a woman," Bedard said.

"But the victims were all sexually assaulted."

"But no semen was found."

"So you think the bodies could've been interfered with in order to direct attention away from the fact that the murderer is a woman?"

"It could be."

"So you think it's a woman?"

"No, I think it's a man, too."

Maggie laughed and smacked playfully Bedard on the shoulder. In that split second, he pulled her to him and kissed her.

She didn't pull away.

Maybe it was the moment of danger or expectation but she let it happen and only when she made herself deliberately conscious of how different this kiss was from Laurent's did she finally stop and push away from Bedard.

She put her hand to her mouth. His face was still close, his eyes glittering and focused on her mouth. She took a step back and felt a vague nausea tremble up from her gut.

"Roger," she said in a hoarse whisper, "please help me make sure that doesn't happen again."

Bedard walked back to the driver's side of the car, pulling his car keys from his jacket pocket.

"Ask me anything else," he said with a smile.

~

A hundred yards away, the old hunter stood with his dog at his heel. The hunter's ears could not pick out the words but his eyes could see.

Oh, yes, Jean-Luc thought, *they could certainly see.*

~

The large king size bed creaked under their weight with each movement. Yves made a mental note to have it replaced. Brigitte had bought it when they were first married. He grimaced at the flourish of quaint, curling wrought iron in the headboard. It was so romantic and ridiculous, he had thought. It was not a style that had ever suited him.

"You are not getting up?" The woman in the bed murmured as she traced a languid finger down his bare back. "I thought you were bringing coffee to me."

Yves shook himself out of his thoughts and turned to his lover. He leaned over and kissed her deeply. "I am just going," he said. "Cream, yes?"

The woman nodded, her pale hair draping the rumpled pillow like a gossamer shroud of gold. "I love you, Yves," she said. Her eyes followed him carefully as he rose from the bed and pulled on his silk dressing gown.

"But, of course, you do," Yves said and lit a cigarette. He smiled at her before leaving the room.

Madeleine could hear him in the kitchen next door. She listened to him assemble a tray of coffee cups and croissants.

Presently, she heard the coffeemaker signaling its finish. She turned and looked out the small bedroom window.

Yves' apartment was situated on the *rue de John F. Kennedy*, which was a quiet street. A pigeon flew to the windowsill and perched there, seeming to inspect Madeleine as if trying to decide whether or not to enter the room.

Finally, the bird flew away. Madeleine heard Yves open the kitchen door to retrieve a cold pitcher of cream.

Soon, she knew, he would return to her.

Laurent carried Zouzou in the crook of his arm. He stood in the middle of his vineyard and surveyed his land.

"Are you late in harvesting this year?" Grace asked.

She tucked the ends of her silk scarf snugly around her head and squinted at the lush vineyard through her sunglasses.

"A little," Laurent admitted.

"It won't be a problem, will it?"

Laurent shook his head.

"The pickers come tomorrow," he said. He kissed the child on the cheek. "Zouzou is such a big girl. And your sister is having fun, too, eh?"

They watched Taylor run to the end of the stonewall that surrounded the field. She turned and waved to them before continuing on at a jog.

"Exercise is good for her," Laurent said.

"Listen, Laurent," Grace said, "you know Maggie is just trying to find her calling over here. It's not easy finding something to do in a foreign country."

Laurent grunted, then handed the child back to Grace.

"She needs a hat," he said with his eyes on Taylor in the distance. "It's still very hot."

"And besides," Grace continued, hoisting Zouzou onto her hip. "You have all this and that's quite consuming, isn't it?"

Laurent looked at Grace as if he expected she meant more by her words.

"I mean, it would be, wouldn't it? Running a vineyard, my goodness."

"You don't need to flatter me, Grace. Just tell me."

Grace sighed. "Darling, I love you dearly, but is there really a reason to go about being the French Country Lunkhead? Hunting, drinking with your mates, stomping about your fields, and spending more time with your dogs than with Maggie?"

Laurent grinned and scratched his head.

"I suppose I asked for this."

"Honestly, Maggie married a sexy, slightly nefarious con man—not that I'm saying that being a criminal was a good thing or anything—not a *farmer*. And I'm not saying give up the vineyard. I'm saying, perhaps you don't need to throw yourself into the life and shoes of the sweaty French peasant with quite so much vigor. Oh, well, Win always tells me to shut up about now. Maggie does too, come to think of it."

"We never spend much time alone, you and I," Laurent said as he examined a branch of plump grapes. Laurent ate a grape, testing it for sweetness, then handed one to Zouzou.

"But you are a special friend not just to Maggie." He threw the stripped branch away. "And I respect your opinion."

"Oh, Laurent, can we hug?"

He laughed and pulled her and the child close.

"Hey, that nasty man is coming! *Maman!*"

Grace frowned as Taylor ran toward them.

"What on earth are you talking about, Taylor?" she asked, shielding the sun from her eyes.

"It's Jean-Luc," Laurent said. He pointed to the north corner of the vineyard. The old man was climbing over the stone wall, preceded by his hunting dog.

"Well, maybe this is a good time to hit the trail," Grace said. "Sometimes Jean-Luc is a little hard to take—even for me." She squeezed Laurent's arm. "Forgive me, darling Laurent. And give Maggie a kiss for me."

"*Ah, oui,*" Laurent said as he watched Jean-Luc's determined approach. "*Bien sûr.*"

The thin chef cinched his apron tighter in one nervous jerk. Aside from that one gesture, he gave no indication that his concentration on a large wad of pastry dough was being affected.

A loud crash echoed throughout the restaurant's kitchen as two metal bowls came tumbling down from the shelf.

August Moreau, standing in the center of the kitchen, raked a tray of ceramic soup bowls to the floor with one sweep of his hand. His face was purple with rage.

"The bastard!" he shouted. "I will cut his heart from his lying throat and serve it to his mother!"

He turned to the chef massaging the dough.

"You are massacring that dough, you idiot! We are not making pizza, moron. Have you seen Yves Genet in my restaurant today? Have you seen him?"

The thin chef looked at his boss with surprise. "*Moi?*"

"*Non*, you *imbécile!* I'm talking to the casserole dishes but you are in my way! Yes, you! Have you seen him?"

The chef wiped his fingers on his apron and looked around as if searching for help.

The *maître 'd,* a tall black man, came into the kitchen.

"Ah, Bennett!" said Moreau. "You've seen him, haven't you?

You've seated the bastard, haven't you? He's here right now, isn't he? I'll kill the bastard!"

"Dr. Genet is not in the restaurant," Bennett said calmly. "I told you I would notify you."

"I *want* him to come!" Moreau shrieked. "I *want* the bastard to eat in my restaurant one last time!"

He snatched up a large chopper and slammed the mound of dough on the counter in front of him. "He will never eat again. I promise you that!"

Throwing the chopper to the floor, Moreau turned and stormed from the kitchen, slamming the door to his office behind him.

The *maître d'* sighed and, without speaking, returned to the dining room. The thin chef held his trembling hands to his stomach, pressing lightly on his knuckles, where the knife had grazed them.

The sky seemed to darken earlier that afternoon as Maggie drove home in the rain on the country roads. She'd called home twice but there was no answer. The combination of the gloomy weather, her confusion over the incident with Bedard, and the fact that she seemed even further from knowing who killed Brigitte manifested themselves in a sour mood of discouragement.

Pleased to see Laurent's Renault in the gravel driveway, Maggie hurriedly parked her car and unsuccessfully dodged the raindrops to the front door.

"Laurent?"

She shook out her damp head scarf. When she entered the house she was surprised to see a lively fire in the hearth.

"My God," she said, following sounds coming from the kitchen. "We've been broken into and the vile buggers have built a fire and are preparing a hot meal. I told you to keep the doors locked."

Petit-Four ran to her from her bed in the kitchen and jumped against Maggie's knees for a moment until Laurent turned from the stove and handed her a glass of rosé.

"Don't ask if it's one of ours. It's not. It's better."

He leaned over and kissed her.

"I can't tell you what a treat it is to come home to this, and oh, that smells so good whatever you're doing in here. And a fire in the fireplace—on such a rainy evening."

"Why don't you get out of your wet things? Dinner isn't for another quarter of an hour. Change and join me in front of the fireplace. I have some things to discuss with you."

"My God. You want a divorce. Are you sure you've given it enough time? I mean, we've only been at this not quite a year."

"I will never understand your humor. Go. Change into dry clothes."

Maggie ran upstairs and peeled off her wet clothes. She kicked them into a sodden pile in the bathroom and pulled on a pair of jeans and a sweater.

Examining herself in the mirror, she ran her fingers through her long hair to let it air dry and hurried back downstairs.

A small tray of hors d'oeuvres sat on the coffee table in front of the fire along with her wine glass and his.

Maggie seated herself in front of the fire and took a long sip of wine. Whatever he was up to, she decided, it didn't have the tenor of trying to soften bad news. She allowed her hopes to rise.

Laurent sat down and picked up his wine glass and took a sip. Then, he put down his glass and picked up her hand.

"I would like to begin," he said, "with a very large apology to you."

Several hours later, as Maggie lay in bed happy and virtually transformed, she allowed herself the luxury of reliving Laurent's words and, more importantly, Laurent's promises of the evening.

Admitting he had abandoned the cookbook project he had originally started with her with the promise to do better was only the first of several startling revelations. After a long discussion, they decided that they would work on the project together and that, unlike most French cookbooks, their cookbook would not strive to depict French cuisine with a bow to Michelin stars but to the love and execution of simple, honest, farmhouse cooking.

Moreover, Laurent apologized for escaping to the vineyard and promised that the cookbook would not take a backseat to his grape fields.

In fact, he vowed neither project would take priority over their life together and their love for each other.

To cap it off, Maggie thought as she rolled over to watch her dozing husband, he *wants to start a family*.

In her mind's eye, Maggie remembered the Laurent she had met three years ago. A con man, yes, with much of his past still a mystery to her and likely to remain so. But a charming, softhearted con man, as likely to rescue his victims as steal from them.

Or, in her case, fall in love with them.

The question she had wanted to ask him all evening however remained silent in her brain. What did it matter what had prompted this loving change of heart? This cataclysmic track-switching?

More than once she had marveled at the irony and coincidence that the same day she had succumbed to a minor infraction of her wedding vows, those same vows had been strengthened and reinforced.

She watched her husband. His eyelids never fluttered and he never moaned in his sleep. He, who surely had so much to trouble and shame him in his life, slept without a doubt or shred of guilt or recrimination.

Self-absolution, Maggie thought, touching the handsome profile with a light finger. *There's nothing quite like it.*

She kissed his lips and got out of their bed. An exquisite early dinner followed by a long evening of talking and love-making had left her hungry.

Maybe I'm pregnant already.

Humming, with a lightness in her heart she assembled a cheese sandwich, spreading *aïoli* on both slices of bread. She dusted off the wooden cutting board and went to slide it back into its space between the counter and she when she heard a rustling sound.

What does Laurent keep in here? He's like a packrat with his kitchen a nest of found treasures and culinary bijoux.

She slipped her hand in the crevice and pulled out a small, heavy package.

Don't tell me he's taken to hiding my Christmas presents already.

She tentatively peeled back the heavy brown paper, knowing she shouldn't and already planning how to look surprised on Christmas morning when her fingers froze.

There in the middle of the butcher-block paper was a black Glock semi-automatic.

12

"What next? Cocoa Puffs?"

Maggie threw Grace an unamused look and continued to pour grits onto Marie's plate.

"Marie specifically asked for a sample of Southern breakfast fare," Maggie replied defensively.

Grace said and patted Marie's hand.

"A word to the wise, darling. Don't get caught hungry south of the Mason-Dixie line if you're ever traveling in the States."

Maggie set the pot of grits down on the table with a thud.

"Are you kidding? Southern food is fantastic! It's nourishing."

"High in fat."

"Totally delicious."

"Cooked to mush."

Marie laughed and put a hand out to touch both of her American friends.

"Stop!" she said. "I am laughing too much to eat."

"That's the point, *chérie*," Grace said. "Honestly, you'll thank me."

"*Non, non,* I want to eat these grits of Maggie's. It is a little like polenta, *oui?*"

"A little, I guess," Maggie said, sliding a couple of fried eggs onto her plate. "Just black coffee for you, I suppose, Gracie?"

"Hell, no. I need to get used to American food again. Load me up!"

They all laughed.

Maggie retreated to the kitchen with the empty pot. She glanced out the kitchen window at the bird feeder that Laurent had put up earlier that morning.

He had left to supervise the harvesting pickers on his field before Grace and Marie arrived.

He told her that he had some ideas for a chapter in the book that revolved around the idea of creating a meal only after one has visited the day's market to see what was fresh.

It wasn't a new idea, but he promised he had a few twists to give it an interesting angle.

So early in the morning for more promises, Maggie caught herself thinking as she kissed him good-bye.

After agonizing consideration that had taken the remainder of her night, Maggie had decided not to mention the gun to Laurent. Their détente was still so fresh and so fragile, that confronting him with this major broken promise would likely do more damage than the broken promise itself.

Maggie needed to dream, and to believe, just a little bit longer in the hope of their future.

"It is so good to laugh again," Marie said.

"It's good to hear you laugh," Grace said.

"How is René?" Maggie asked as she placed toast and bacon on Grace's plate. "I guess he's pretty discouraged."

Marie shook her head.

"My René is usually so cynical, yes?" she said. "But for some reason, he has decided to believe that the stupid police will get it right in the end. After all, as he says, he didn't kill Brigitte. They can't convict him if he's innocent, eh?"

The tone of Marie's voice exposed her own opinion.

"We'll get him out, I promise," Maggie said.

"She will too," Grace said between forkfuls. "This is really delicious, Maggie. You ought to do short order."

"It's the extent of my abilities in the kitchen," Maggie said, seating herself. "I do a great American breakfast."

"It is really quite good," Marie agreed. "I bet August would love it."

Maggie flashed a quick look at Grace. "Speaking of August."

Marie put down her fork. "He is many things," she said. "I have known him for so long. Known him to be capable of many surprises."

"But not murder?" Maggie said.

"Before we indict all the members of my family," Marie said, "I have something to tell you that might start pointing the finger in other directions, eh?"

Marie got up from the table, retrieved her purse from the living room sofa, and extracted a small notebook, which she placed next to Maggie's plate.

"Brigitte's gardening diary," she said. "She left it at my house. Open it to the day she died."

Maggie picked the diary up and flipped to the last week in July. Her eyes widened.

"Interesting, *non?*" Marie said.

"What?" Grace asked. "What does it say?"

"Why does Brigitte have dinner engagements written in a garden diary?" Maggie asked.

"Dinner?" Grace asked. "Does it say she's rendezvousing with August that day?"

"No," Maggie said, handing the diary to Grace. "It says she's meeting Madeleine for lunch that day."

Grace looked at the diary entry and frowned.

"Is that bad?" she asked.

"*Non,*" Marie answered for Maggie. "Unless you have carefully avoided mentioning the fact, even after your luncheon partner shows up dead."

The pickers were still moving methodically through the rows of grape loaded vines. Maggie had spent much of the afternoon preparing lemonade, cold tea, beer and sandwiches for them and watching their progress from the back garden.

Bushels of grapes were now lined up on the front drive and stacked on the front terrace awaiting the trucks from *Cortier & Fils* to arrive. The grapes would be processed through the co-op. Half of the bottles sold for *Domaine St-Buvard* through the co-op and the other half returned to *Domaine St-Buvard* for Laurent's wine cellar.

Maggie picked up her laptop and settled on the couch. From where she sat she could see the workers bent to their backbreaking task in the hot autumn. She could see Laurent walking up and down the rows of vines as he directed and encouraged his workers.

Wasn't there a small domestic crisis immediately after his promise to dispose of the handgun?

Maggie tried hard to remember.

Didn't one of the dogs come in with an injured snout or bloody paw or something? And perhaps, in the distracting flurry of tending to the hurt dog, Laurent had just tucked the gun away until he could deal with it later? And then possibly he'd just forgotten he hadn't taken care of it?

Maggie opened a new document on her computer and keyed in the list of ingredients for the ricotta and herb-stuffed ravioli Laurent had dictated to her earlier that afternoon. She made a note to ask him if they should suggest types of wines for these recipes.

Another worker came to the door asking for water and Maggie got up to get it for him. He said he'd worked through lunch, so Maggie also handed him a couple of the egg and pepper sandwiches that she and Laurent had prepared that morning. Muttering his thanks, the man returned to his work.

Maggie got herself a Coke and stood in the doorway watching the pickers move steadily toward the eastern quadrant of the field. They'd been picking steadily for two days. Laurent thought they might finish today.

On impulse, Maggie picked up her cellphone and punched in Madeleine Dupré's number. It was answered immediately.

"*Allo?*"

"Madeleine?"

"Maggie, hello! I'm so happy to hear from you."

"I've been so busy, what with the harvest and all," Maggie said. "I was hoping to reconnect with you, maybe over lunch? Say, tomorrow?"

"Tomorrow is gorgeous for seeing you!" Madeleine said. "We must get this friendship off the ground, as you Americans say, *n'est-ce pas?*"

"Absolutely. How about at the hospital? I've got to be in the area anyway."

"In Nîmes?"

"Yeah, I haven't seen Pijou yet and I told Marie I'd stop in. Plus, I have something of Yves's I've been meaning to return."

Maggie thought there was an awkward pause before Madeleine spoke.

"Something of Yves's?" she said.

"Nothing important. So, what do you say? Noon? Straight up?"

"Straight up is good with me, Maggie," Madeleine said, no warmth in her voice now. "The only way I'd have it."

"Great, see you tomorrow."

"*Absolument.*"

The next morning was cold, the first really chilly day of the season. Laurent announced at breakfast that it was a good omen that the harvest had been completed just before the first cold weather.

Ignoring a temptation to ask him when he had started believing in omens, Maggie found herself grateful the harvest was behind them for another year. The annual invasion of impoverished grape-pickers made her uncomfortable. It made her feel too much like a privileged landowner.

"We celebrate tonight, eh?" Laurent said over a breakfast of *café au lait,* French bread, jam, American bacon and Special-K cereal.

"By we, I guess you don't mean only Maggie and Laurent," Maggie said good-naturedly.

"You will come, surely?" Laurent said. "It is our triumph together, *n'est-ce pas?* Our accomplishment?"

"Would you be totally devastated if I begged off? I mean, no one's happier than I am about the grapes being all picked and I'm sure it'll be a great wine and all, but if you're going to stay out half the night with Jean-Luc and the guys..."

"It will be mostly men," Laurent admitted.

"Yeah, see, I think I'd like to take a long bath and curl up in front of the TV with one of those videos you don't really like."

Laurent got up from the table and kissed her.

"We will celebrate later together," he said.

She laughed. "That's a date. But probably not later *tonight!*"

He grinned.

An hour and a half later, Maggie parked her car in the hospital parking lot in Nîmes and walked to the outdoor bistro across the street. Madeleine was already at a table waiting for her.

"*Bonjour,* Maggie!"

The two women greeted each other with a kiss on the cheek. Madeleine wore a gold necklace with a tiny cluster of diamond chips swinging from a slim, gold tether.

"You are a little late," Madeleine said.

"Yeah, sorry," Maggie signaled to the waiter. "Have you looked at the menu?"

"I have decided I am not so very hungry," Madeleine said. She lit a cigarette.

The waiter approached the table. "*Oui, Madame?*"

"*Deux cafés,*" Madeleine said. The waiter departed.

"Madeleine, I have a date book of Brigitte's that says she had lunch with you the day she died."

Madeleine's expression did not change. She blew a shaky circle of smoke into the air between them.

"I had no lunch plans with Brigitte for that day."

"Kind of weird she'd have you down in her book, then, isn't it? Something like this could be considered downright admissible, you know."

"'Admissible?'"

"Something that's acceptable as evidence in a court of law. I'm saying this diary information might be damning for you."

"It means nothing, Maggie." Madeleine stubbed out her cigarette and smiled at the waiter who set down two cups of coffee. "I am not responsible for what Brigitte wrote in her diary. It does not mean it is the truth. It does not mean she did not make a mistake. Perhaps she meant the Tuesday before?"

"She had a dentist appointment the Tuesday before."

"I see. You have decided I killed Brigitte? Too bad. I had hoped we could be friends."

"I had hoped that too," Maggie said. "But friends don't lie to each other."

"*Au contraire, chérie,*" Madeleine said, pulling out a Clarins tube and reapplying her lipstick. She looked sadly at Maggie. "That's all the very best ones do."

An hour later, Maggie was walking the hospital corridors, frustrated and impatient. It had been a long drive for nothing, she thought.

Madeleine insisted she had not met Brigitte that day. She seemed more interested in why Maggie wanted to see Yves Genet than in clearing her own name.

Maggie was deeply disappointed because she had hoped that the interview with Madeleine would answer her questions about the woman—at least enough to believe she could still value her as a friend.

One thing Maggie did know from her hour with Madeleine was that Madame Dupré knew more than she was saying. And Maggie was sure that the information Madeleine possessed was as unpleasant as it would be enlightening.

Maggie stopped at the nurses station on the third floor and asked if Dr. Genet was on the floor. She received an indifferent shrug from the nurse. Annoyed, Maggie walked the length of the nursing floor and peeked into patients' rooms in search of a white coat.

Genet had had no qualms about mentioning August to her last time she was here and she intended to ask him directly if he had set August up on a fake rendezvous with Brigitte. If so, why? And if not, then why would August lie about it?

It might yield her nothing, but Maggie had discovered that some of the littlest things—and what often appeared to be a monumental waste of time—often delivered a nugget of information that was pure gold. And since it was obvious the police couldn't be bothered ferreting out the gold dust in this case, Maggie was only too happy to ask the questions, look in the drawers, and sniff around behind the cupboards.

If asked why she was on the floor, she was fully prepared to play the dunce tourist in search of a friend hurt in a car accident.

As she turned at the solarium at the end of the hall, she spotted the door to the linen closet where Yves had endured her questions the week before. She rapped loudly on the door. There was no answer but when she tried the knob the door swung open.

She stepped in and closed the door behind her. Even though Yves had used this room as a sexual meeting place on the day of Brigitte's death, Maggie was sure Bedard's men had not carefully examined it.

Still, not really knowing what she was looking for, Maggie went to the shelves with the stacks of stiffly pressed sheets. She slid her fingers under each sheet and lifted each one by one. She wasn't sure what she was looking for.

Next she turned her attention to the examination table. It had a hard plastic cover, easy to wipe down, with connecting hooks for the long rolls of paper that would cover the top for each new patient examined. She knelt and looked under the table.

Instantly, she saw it. A gold earring with a cluster of diamond chips. An earring with the same setting as the necklace she had seen around Madeleine's neck at lunch. She picked up the earring

So Madeleine is still boffin' Yves—which explains her discomfort in my trying to track him down. Not very pretty behavior, chérie, coming from Brigitte's best friend.

For a brief moment, Maggie felt a wave of panic unattached to anything she could see or feel. In that wave, she also felt an unsettling desire to talk to Bedard. Shaking off the feeling, she tucked the earring into the pocket of her slacks and resumed her search.

She jerked open the medicine cabinet door, found the

cabinet empty, and went back to lifting the stacks of linens to see if anything else was wedged under or between them.

She heard a group of nurses walking down the hall and stop right outside the linen room door. They appeared to be in good spirits.

Probably just back from lunch.

They soon dispersed and she was left to finish her search in peace.

She wanted to get home before Laurent left for his evening. She wanted to give him an incentive that might dissuade him from being out too very late tonight.

With this thought in mind, she hurriedly checked the rest of the stacks of sheets, then knelt down to stick her hand between two stacks which seemed to have toppled backward off the shelf. When she did, she felt something rubbery and wet.

Gross! I've probably just stuffed my hand into something toxic and infectious.

Drawing her hand out, she was shocked to see it was covered with blood. At first, she thought she had cut herself somehow, but quickly, it became clear the blood was not hers.

Pulling the stacks apart with both hands now, something long and hard shot out between them, hitting her across the side of the face.

It was a human arm.

13

"The pharmacist is bereft."

Bedard leaned forward in the chair facing Maggie. They were sitting in the nurses' medical room with the door closed. The examination room entranceway was criss-crossed with yellow warning tape and its interior crowded with forensic specialists and the hospital's own coroner. They had found the rest of Yves Genet's body.

Maggie shook the image of Yves' lifeless body from her mind. She concentrated on the bridge of Roger Bedard's nose.

"*Jean-Paul* is bereft?" she asked.

"Seems he was in love with Genet."

"God, was there someone *not* sleeping with Yves?"

"Oh, I don't think it was a consummated sort of love."

Bedard's eyes locked with Maggie's.

"Oh well, then," she said, looking away.

There was a knock at the door and one of Bedard's men stuck his head in.

"Do you want to see the body again?" he asked.

Bedard looked at Maggie and shook his head. "At the autopsy."

After Bedard's man left, Maggie forced herself to sit up and away from Bedard.

"I'm okay, really. It was just a shock is all."

"If you were not looking for bodies, *chérie,* what were you looking for in there?"

"Don't call me that, Roger," Maggie said.

Laurent calls me that.

"I was just looking for anything. For a clue, for something that might tell me something. I found Madeleine's earring. It tells me she was still sleeping with him after she swore she wasn't. It tells me she lied."

"You knew that already."

"Proof is always nice, don't you think?"

Bedard sighed and leaned back in his chair. He continued to watch Maggie closely.

"Am I really the one you should be questioning?" Maggie asked. "I mean, wouldn't it make more sense to try to find the person who killed Yves? And why are you back on the case anyway?"

Bedard shrugged. "There is an argument to be made that this is a different case. It's certainly a different murder. But, you're right. I've been reinstated."

"It's not at all a different case and you know that. But you're back in charge because of the information I gave you, aren't you?"

"Not at all."

"Liar. Do you think I killed Yves?"

"Don't be ridiculous."

"Well, while we sit here the killer gets further away."

"Maggie, the body has been in there for hours. That room is not frequently used. The killer was gone long before you arrived. Do you think he is lurking in the Men's room waiting for us all to go away?" Bedard laughed playfully.

"I should think smug condescension would be the *last* thing you would try on me," Maggie said hotly, "considering the examples of your past police work on this case. And Connor Mackensie's too now that I think of it. That was your case, too, right?"

Bedard's smile faded and he shifted uncomfortably.

"Look, I'm sorry. You're right. I'm being oafish, and so far you have been the only one coming up with any real clues. But we have the murder scene and the body now. We cannot stop and question everyone in the hospital. Surely, you see this."

Maggie rubbed her eyes wearily.

"In Atlanta, they'd have the whole damn block cordoned off and everybody stuck here until a cop had personally asked them where they were at the time of the murder. I can't believe how relaxed your methods are."

Bedard stood up and eased the tension out of his back.

"You didn't touch the body?"

"Except for briefly shaking hands with it, no."

"You didn't move it?"

"I told you, no."

"Why were you in Nîmes today?"

"I had a lunch date with Madeleine."

"Who you think is a liar."

"It wasn't for pleasure. I found a note in Brigitte's diary that she planned to have lunch with Madeleine the day she died, only Madeleine never mentioned the fact to anyone."

"You have Brigitte Genet's personal *diary?*"

"I just got it yesterday."

"And you arranged lunch with Madame Dupré to confront her about the luncheon engagement. I thought we were supposed to tell each other when we got information."

"I'm telling you now."

"I'll remember that. Time lapse information. Well, you can go then, I guess. I'll call you if there's anything else."

"Oh, come on, Roger. " Maggie laughed. "This is pouting in

any language! I'm sorry I didn't call you and tell you about the diary, but I told you right away when I discovered a corpse, now, didn't I?"

Roger snorted in exasperation.

"It must be a cultural thing. I don't know when you're joking."

Maggie picked up her bag and walked to the door.

"Funny," she said. "That's what Laurent always says. You'll call me at home with the autopsy results?"

Bedard nodded, as Maggie left the room.

Madeleine held her breath from where she stood outside the double swinging doors of the intensive care unit. Her face was contorted into an ugly smile.

The police are so stupid. Instead of questioning me about Yves's death, they actually offered their condolences!

She remembered the look of bewildered pain on Richard's face when the police told them of Yves's death.

It was true, she thought coldly. *The poor idiot loved Yves as a brother. Perhaps he will be the only person to truly mourn the bastard's passing.*

She peered through the small window opening of the door to make sure that the inhabitant's attendants were occupied elsewhere, then pushed open the door into the hospital room which held the unconscious Pijou.

Her hands squeezed her Prada reptile clutch so tightly she could feel the spine snap beneath her fingers.

Perhaps, again, there is still one more left who may also mourn.

"I'm telling you, Grace, I'm convinced that Madeleine killed Yves," Maggie said into her cell phone.

She stood inside the hospital cafeteria and squinted through the large picture window at the rain pouring down outside. With the traditionally terrible phone reception she knew she didn't stand a chance of getting through if she tried to make a call on her drive home.

Besides, her cell phone battery was nearly dead—probably good for this one last call.

"But I thought you said they were having an affair," Grace said on her end.

"They were. You know how upsetting those can be."

Grace laughed.

Maggie caught the eye of Jean-Paul Remey as he went through the line in the cafeteria. He turned his red-rimmed eyes away from her.

"Marie says Uncle August was making threats against Yves in his restaurant," Grace said. "Maybe it was him?"

"Well, let's face it," Maggie said. "Nobody liked Yves. Hell, it could've been any one of his nurses, for that matter. Is Marie with you?"

"Yes, she's spending the night. I'm going with her to court tomorrow in Aix for René's hearing. Hold on a second."

Marie's voice came on the line. "Hello, Maggie?"

"Hey, Marie."

"I just wanted to tell you that sometimes to not think about something for a little bit is to finally see the thing you have been looking for all along, you understand?"

"Yeah, okay. Thanks, Marie."

"Also, like with painting, You need to see the whole picture as it hangs on the wall—from the distance, yes? Do not get overwhelmed by the details! Look at the whole picture."

"Yes, all right."

Grace got back on the line.

"Listen, darling, why don't you come by? It's just us girls tonight, Win is in Paris working out the last part of his deal on selling the software business. It will be fun."

"Thanks, but no. Laurent is out tonight and I really feel a

need to spend some time alone, you know? Take a bath, paint my toenails, give myself a facial, maybe give Mother a call."

"I perfectly understand. The full female pampering treatment. Good for you."

"Give Marie my love, okay? And thank her for the advice and tell René to hang in there. At least they can't accuse him of killing Yves."

"I will, darling. Enjoy tonight."

Twenty minutes later, after grabbing a cafeteria sandwich and a cup of coffee, Maggie was back in her car heading home. She spotted Bedard's car in the hospital parking lot as she drove out. She knew the body had been moved. Maybe her words got through to him and he was still here asking if anybody saw anything?

Buoyed by the idea that Roger might be trying to tighten up what, up to now, had been exceedingly sloppy detective work, Maggie resolved to put the whole case out of her mind for one night.

She drove two miles in the increasingly fierce rain before thoughts of Yves and Brigitte came inevitably back to her.

She never did reconcile how Brigitte could have married Yves in the first place.

Either Yves had demonically evolved from the person he'd been when Brigitte married him to the monster he'd become, or Maggie just didn't know Brigitte and her pathology well enough to be surprised by her loving him.

She tried to imagine Laurent changing so completely from the man she fell in love with to something resembling the creature that Yves was. And when she did, she knew that Yves must have been venal from the beginning.

How could Brigitte have been so stupid? Had she been so

shallow that Yves's looks and stature as a physician blinded her to his true nature? Was this the woman Maggie was considering as her next soul mate? Or was it something other than myopia?

Was there, in fact, something about Brigitte herself that was attracted to Yves specifically because of who he was? Maybe she hated herself and felt she needed to be abused?

Was she atoning for something?

Maggie's mind raced to the men in Brigitte's childhood—René and August Moreau.

Could something have happened between "uncle" and "niece" when Brigitte was a child?

She took the ramp to the D999 and saw she was low on gas. The clock on the dashboard said it was after seven o'clock.

How could it have gotten so late? Laurent will already have left for his evening's celebrations.

She wished now that she'd called him from the hospital and told him what was going on.

What *is* going on, she wondered?

She thought of Bedard, so handsome, but so different from Laurent. Solid and wiry and ready to spring on every comment or askance look or gesture she might make, as opposed to Laurent's steady, unblinking, slow observation-without-comment approach to life.

It was like the difference between a terrier with lots of personality and speed, and a St-Bernard, strong, and steady—but full of quiet cunning. Maggie blinked.

Is that how she really saw Laurent? Full of guile under all that reserve?

Well, as a con man, he did used to lie for a living, she reminded herself. But was it against his nature to do so?

She brought a picture of Laurent to mind and saw him, big and good-looking, his lips full, a wry smile often there, his eyes dark brown, his pupils nonexistent. She had looked into those unfathomable dark eyes so many times in the past few years and always found answers, reassurance, love and yes, secrets.

Will there always be secrets between us?

On the off chance he might have left the house late, Maggie pulled out her cell phone to see if she had any power at all. The battery was completely dead.

Sighing, she tossed it back into her purse and accelerated, keeping her eye on the low fuel gauge. He was probably already gone anyway, she told herself. The evening was dark and the rain was coming down hard. She would be glad to get home.

She tried to remember how Brigitte and Yves met. Obviously she'd been attracted to his looks first. Maggie thought of Madeleine and had to give her begrudging respect for having married Richard. She had been the wiser of the two French women in the matter of the heart.

Or had she? Although arguably the better of the two men, Richard was not the right choice for Madeleine or why was she screwing around on him?

Maggie had overheard the staff nurses discussing Richard, the gist being that he was very nice but dull.

Did Madeleine kill Yves? Why would she? They were still lovers. Was one of them trying to leave the affair? Did one of them make a terrible discovery? Bedard said Yves had been stabbed with a scalpel.

Maggie drew a tired hand across her face and punched on the radio. Static assailed her as she tried without success to tune in a nearby station. Finally, she turned the radio off. She was still about thirty minutes from her driveway.

When she got home, she planned on dropping her wet clothes in the foyer as she entered, pulling on a robe before feeding the dogs and lighting a fire. Although she wasn't hungry, she knew Laurent would have left something for her either warming in the oven or wrapped up on the kitchen counter. He would have decanted a bottle of wine for her too.

What about August? Is he just a big powder-puff or could he have killed Yves?

He seemed so afraid and respectful of Yves. Could he have made the switch to violent hatred? He adored Brigitte. But surely he must have been aware that Yves was hurting her?

Maggie exited the D999 onto the remote country road that led to St-Buvard.

Some people can talk themselves into not believing things they don't want to believe.

Surely, Bedard will get a statement from August as to his whereabouts at the time of the murder.

Either his people at the restaurant will give him his alibi, or we've got our suspect.

She made a mental note to call Bedard when she got home. A tiny rattling sound pinged up at Maggie from the floorboards or just behind her seat. Annoyed that the car was making new and worrisome noises that would probably warrant a week's visit to the garage in Aix, Maggie twisted the radio knob in hopes it might have come from there. The noise stopped.

It seemed to her that Jean-Paul had been taken off the suspect list pretty quickly.

Just because he's gay and acts like he's sorry that the victim is dead, is that a reason to believe he didn't kill him?

Maggie shook her head.

These French were so wrapped up in their sophisticated version of sexual implications that they can't stand to think that sex might not be a motive.

For that matter, if a gay man attracted to Yves could want him dead for some reason, couldn't a gay man who also happened to despise women want Brigitte dead? Was it possible that Brigitte was killed—not because of who she was intrinsically—but because she stood in the way of someone else? Someone who would kill, not from jealousy or desire or passion, but from revenge and resentment?

What if you took the sex out of it?

Maggie found herself energized by this new line. The details of the case seemed to be falling away, blending into a pattern that formed a picture. If she could just step back from it in her mind and watch it develop.

Forget the question of who hated Yves. Everyone hated him!

Maybe the better question was who could like a scumbag like Yves?

When he wasn't bragging about the women he slept with, he was condescending and cold. What friend would tolerate or trust him?

Why did Richard? He not only liked Yves, he defended him. What did Richard see to like in him? Was Richard just too pure? Too good that he couldn't see evil when he was staring into its face?

Maggie left behind the dark, winding road that threaded through the village of St-Buvard. The shutters had been pulled shut, the vegetable bins and postcard carousels safely tucked away for the night. No light showed through the tightly fastened windows to indicate that the village was anything but deserted.

She slowed the car to drive the painstaking switchbacks on the road leading away from the village.

The thought occurred to her as she negotiated a particularly tricky stretch of gravel that hugged a small bridge with no protective barrier that surely Richard in all the years of his friendship with Yves must have seen Yves for the snake he was.

A chill began to vibrate at the base of Maggie's spine.

Richard knew that Yves was abusing Brigitte.

Richard would have to be an idiot not to see who Yves really was. And Richard was not an idiot. He was a brilliant physician, admired and respected for his specialized knowledge, his analytical mind, and his ability to make astute judgments.

From around the last dark bend in the corkscrew country road, Maggie saw the lights of *Domaine St-Buvard*. Laurent was not home, but he'd left a light on for her.

What if Madeleine wasn't lying about the lunch engagement with Brigitte? What if Brigitte believed she was meeting Madeleine because someone she trusted had set it up?

And who would she trust more than the husband of her friend?

"Madeleine is busy all morning, Brigitte, but she wanted me to ask you to meet her for lunch tomorrow. A nice little place in the country. We were there this weekend—so charming. "

A sickening hard knot formed in Maggie's stomach as the realization hit her.

It's Richard.

Richard knew Yves was screwing Madeleine. So he raped and killed Yves's wife. When that wasn't enough, he killed Yves, too.

Maggie brought an image to mind of Richard's plain, open face. His eyes were trusting and kind. His homely, unassuming face was a mask covering the calculated expressions and lies.

He's the one with motive, the one no one bothered to query for an alibi, the one with easy access and opportunity.

Maggie's hands gripped the steering wheel. She glanced at her dead cell phone.

Yves was killed with a knife. A surgeon's knife.

Pijou was attacked in her apartment by someone she knew.

The nurse killed earlier this summer was from Yves's hospital.

He's killing all the women Yves desired.

Suddenly, she heard the noise again.

This time, it sounded like a creak or groan as if metal was pushing against leather. This time, Maggie did not reach for the radio knob or curse the fact that the car would be heading for the shop.

Coupled with an escalating terror as she drove to the vacant driveway of her home, she had a logical explanation for the noise.

Someone was in the car with her.

14

Maggie's hands tightened on the steering wheel. The farmhouse was only a hundred yards away. Her mind whirled in a vortex of noise and confusion and she tried hard to hear her own thoughts.

Stop the car now! Jump out and run for it! He's hiding. He's not looking. He won't expect it. Someone will see the car abandoned in the middle of the road. No one comes down this road at this time of night.

Maggie snapped off the car's ignition, leaving the headlights on and jerked the driver's side door open. Her fingers felt slippery and clumsy. She felt like everything was happening in slow motion.

She instantly stumbled on the gravel rocks on the drive and lost one of her clogs. Behind her, she could hear him struggling to open the rear car door. Kicking the other shoe off, she ran for the house, praying, praying, praying.

The light over the front door shone a wedge of light into the darkness. Laurent was not home. Inside was only a little dog and many dark, empty rooms.

Maggie ran toward her home—to the place she would be safe.

She was nearly on the front steps. She saw her reflection in the etched glass double doors. But she could also see the shadow behind her and how close he was. And she knew there was no way.

She wrapped her hand around the front door handle but there was no time to get her keys, to unlock it. Terror fluttered up into her throat. She heard his labored breathing as he barreled up the steps behind her.

An image flashed into her mind of an evening earlier in the fall when she and Laurent had sat here in wicker chairs sipping *pastis* and watching the falling stars. A magical moment on a clear Provençal night.

Then she felt the terrible strength of Richard's cold hands on her neck.

~

The rain had begun by the time Bedard picked up his jacket and left the hospital. A thick fog hovered over the parking lot misting raindrops like a malfunctioning automated car wash. Bedard threw his jacket in the backseat of his car and surveyed the nearly empty parking lot.

He'd left two men to protect the crime scene and sent everyone else on their way--either back to the lab with their goodies or home.

He glanced at his watch. It was too late for Nicole. She'd have been asleep hours by now. He drove back to his apartment and watched the intensifying rainfall force motorists into more careful habits.

Maggie had been right, of course. The police work had not been good. His men had missed much. He himself had not ordered important tests and had failed to insist on certain samples being collected. It was just a job. It was just someone else's daughter being carried away on a stretcher. Someone else's grief and pain. Someone else's need and agony.

He tapped a finger against the steering wheel. As once it had been his own.

I'm in the wrong business.

I don't care enough. I care too much.

He drove to the parking lot of his apartment building and turned off the car. He looked up at the fourth floor window of his apartment. The light was on. Nicole's sitter Naomi was probably watching *Grey's Anatomy* or reruns of some other American TV show. The television faces always showed American intensity and openness, but the voices were comforting, veiled dubbed French. It made him think of Maggie and he smiled.

Interesting how the words are the same. But the interpretation is oh, so different.

A car honked its horn as it sped by and Bedard doused his headlights. Does it make the women any less dead? he wondered. Or their terror any less? To find any of these monsters in Arles or Chicago, one needed to study their crimes, imagine their lives, picture their habits.

One needed to crawl into their nasty, spume-coated heads and live there.

Bedard remembered a line from a song from the early seventies: "To Know You is to Love You." A criminal psychologist had come out a few years later with a study that confirmed that even when the object of one's study was revolting and despicable—hardened criminals and serial killers, for example —those whose job it was to understand them often came, as a result of their intense focus, to care for and even like their subjects.

The thought made Bedard's stomach flop painfully.

To unearth the clues and then to read them well enough to

follow them to where they led, one needed to come face to face with evil.

That was his job. That was his nine-to-five. *And that,* Bedard thought as his eyes moved to his motherless daughter's darkened bedroom window, *was a place I never want to go again.*

His car phone rang and he let it ring until he'd stubbed out his cigarette. *"Oui?"* he said into the handset.

"We've found something," his sergeant said mechanically.

Laurent stubbed out his cigarette and, without obvious movement, motioned for the waiter and the bill.

Jean-Luc frowned. "Surely, you are not leaving?" he said.

Laurent shrugged. "I need to be home."

"But the new *potager*. We haven't discussed how you would replant it."

Laurent shook his head. "

Already I have asked too much advice, taken too much time from you. I will design and build my own kitchen garden."

"Non, non." Jean-Luc put his rough, weather-battered hand on Laurent's larger one. "I want to do this for you, Laurent. It is for me."

"The debt is paid, Jean-Luc."

"For me, never," Jean-Luc said. "I want to do it. I must do it. Only I can plan such a masterful *potager* for you. You have it facing the east sun. The cabbages are buried under the sunflowers. Your wife will plant her azaleas amongst the rose bushes."

Jean-Luc looked up quickly at Laurent but Laurent waved away the man's guilty look.

"Maggie does not hate you, old friend," he said, and then paused. "And I would be glad of your help. Thank you."

Laurent signaled to the waiter to bring a menu and two

more *pastis* while Jean-Luc began to draw on the café napkin the tidy triangles and rectangles of the new kitchen garden.

Only this morning, she had held that creamer in her hands. Secure and comfortable in her own kitchen and in her own house. Laughing with Laurent over something, she couldn't quite remember what.

Now she stared at the creamer. The same creamer, no doubt filled with the same milk from her morning breakfast. Only now, nothing else was the same. Her life, what she had left of it, certainly wasn't.

Richard sat next to her on the sofa. He held a large hunting knife in one hand and rubbed the edge mindlessly with his thumb as he spoke. Maggie cradled little Petit-Four on her lap. She stared alternately at the little creamer and the big knife.

"I am sorry to have startled you," Richard said, reaching over to tousle the ears of Petit-Four. "He's certainly the little protector, isn't he? If he and I become friends, then I will not be needing to kill him after I kill you. I like dogs."

Maggie felt her lunch edging up into her throat and she willed herself not to be sick. She willed herself not to do anything that might rush Richard into action.

A part of her brain found a sliver of hope in the idea that if she did nothing, perhaps he would do nothing. She let him talk.

"I killed Brigitte because her husband was screwing my wife. You know about that, yes?"

Why didn't you just kill Yves? Maggie wanted to scream.

"And I guess I thought it would help," he said tiredly. "I did punish her before I killed her..."

Maggie fought to keep her face expressionless.

"And the other nurse...the one that Yves had been with...

Why are you not talking? You talk so much normally. Do you find all this so boring?"

Maggie shook her head, trying not to stare at the knife.

"Well, you are not speaking."

Maggie licked her lips. "I am afraid."

Richard nodded with satisfaction. "So were the others. That is my only regret. I had to take Yves by surprise. I did not see his fear. Ironic, no? The very one I was doing it for?"

Richard stood. "I never have had such luxury of time before. I think I may be...what do you think?...a little creative tonight?"

Maggie felt the words push past her lips before she could stop them: "My husband will be home any minute."

Richard brought his face close to hers and screamed.

"A lie! A total lie and you, a liar like each one of them! I heard you talking on the phone at the hospital, you stupid, lying bitch! No one is coming tonight. You. Are. Mine."

Maggie clutched the dog, the hope draining from her as she stared into Richard's face, the face of someone who was going to end her life, make her mother grieve, make Laurent rage and weep. Being quiet wasn't going to change or help a damn thing.

She pulled her face back from his and could see again on the dining room table the sweet little Limoge creamer that she and Laurent had bought together in a Paris flea market. It didn't matter what she did now.

She could throw up, cry, beg or attack him physically. It was all going to happen as it had happened before...to Brigitte, to Pijou...to that poor nurse.

Richard straightened up again. He smiled at her as if he could read her thoughts.

"After you," he said, scratching his head as if mulling over a logical problem, "I will kill the other American woman, and Marie, of course, and then Madeleine. And do you know why I will be able to do all this?"

"Because the police are so stupid?"

Richard looked at her as if at a dim, but surprising, pupil.

"Why, yes," he said. "I suppose they are rather stupid."

"And of course, you are so brilliant."

Richard flicked the edge of the knife hard, drawing his own blood across its blade.

"Perhaps I will not indulge in conversation next time," he said, thoughtfully.

"You mean the next time you try to kill someone," Maggie said.

Richard laughed. "Oh, *mon chou!*" he said. "There will be no *attempt*. Oh, you think you have a chance? That you may outfox me?"

Maggie's thoughts crisscrossed inside her brain. She was going to die. Laurent had not done the breakfast dishes. She had not allowed Petit-Four to relieve herself and the dog was fidgeting.

Except for Yves, Richard hadn't killed the others with a knife. She still had her coat on. She was hungry. She was going to die. Maybe Bedard would call. Maybe Grace would drop by. Maybe Richard would fall down dead of a heart attack.

"I have to walk the dog," she said, licking her dry lips.

Richard held the knife to the poodle's small head.

"I can save both of us the bother of ever having to walk the dog," he said with a smile.

Maggie resisted the urge to clutch the dog into her coat—a move she was sure would promote its immediate destruction.

"I thought you liked dogs," she said.

"You're right. I do." He took the dog from Maggie's hands, walked to the garden door and set her outside. He returned and motioned Maggie to stand.

"I don't imagine she will be going for the sheriff, eh? Like your Lassie or Rin-Tin-tin?" He giggled expansively over his American trivia knowledge.

Maggie stood slowly. Her hands were wet with perspiration and she wiped them against her coat.

"Remove the coat," Richard said, wagging the knife at her.

Maggie unbuttoned her coat and slipped out of it.

"Put it on the couch," he said.

She did, feeling nearly as naked in her skirt and sweater as she she felt getting up from a bath. He handed her a black marker he had taken from his jacket pocket.

"Usually I do this part myself," he said.

She took the marker.

"Draw a large X across your face," he said.

Maggie hesitated.

"It is very simple. Not hard to do."

She thought, for one mad moment, of telling him to go ahead and kill her but the words wouldn't come.

"Come on. Shall I do it, after all?"

Maggie put the pen to her forehead and forced herself to draw the nib downward across her nose and cheeks. Her stomach lurched and she thought she might vomit.

When she finished, she dropped the marker to the couch. He scooped it up and put it in his pocket.

"Mustn't leave presents for the police, eh?" He grinned and then lazily waved his knife at her. "In the kitchen. I'm hungry."

Maggie's mind, jumbled one second with conflicting images and thoughts and frozen the next with fear and disbelief, seemed to suddenly converge into one searing, blazing light.

The confusion of thoughts fell to the wayside with the utterance of those three words: *into the kitchen*.

She moved slowly, afraid to let him know by any movement or involuntary facial muscle that she had found a glimmer of hope and direction amongst the terror.

She was not going to be slain where she sat on the sofa amongst her Egyptian pillows and Pashmina throws. She was to be given a glimpse of an opportunity.

And if she worked it right, it would be enough.

The Glock was in the kitchen.

Bedard frowned at the paper bag sitting on his desk. "Where did you find it?" he asked.

The sergeant stood across from him and chewed a dirty fingernail. "Housekeeping found it, sir."

"I didn't ask you who found it, Sergeant."

He should be happy. He didn't feel happy, but really, he must be. It was, after all, the murder weapon.

"In the laundry, sir," the sergeant answered. "He didn't even bother to wipe it clean. We sent the blood samples to the lab—"

"They will match up," Bedard said. "Perhaps the man's ego will be such that he did not bother to wipe his prints either. Finally, we have the bastard."

"Well," the sergeant shifted from foot to food. "Perhaps it is not unusual to find a bloody scalpel in a hospital. Sir."

Bedard looked up at the sergeant for the first time since he entered the room. The man actually cared about looking competent, Bedard realized with a surprise. The sergeant was trying to cover for himself.

"Sergeant," Bedard said, not unkindly. "Are you a complete moron or do you honestly believe that surgeons traditionally dispose of their operating equipment by tossing them into the hospital laundry after use?"

"I am not aware of how the knife got there," the sergeant replied. His face was shiny and red.

"I know you're not," Bedard said, rubbing his tired eyes with his hand and wondering why recovery of the murder weapon did not delight him. "That will be all, Sergeant. Good work."

He squeezed the last two words out like trapped air from a

balloon. The sergeant turned to leave and then stopped at the door.

"Oh, there was one more thing, sir."

She held the baguette on the chopping board and carefully sliced off four large pieces of bread with the serrated bread knife. Richard stood by her side and held his large butcher knife to her chin.

"Your hands tremble," he said to her. "Mind you don't cut yourself." He giggled.

Maggie put the bread knife down. "What do you want on your sandwich?"

"What do you have?"

Maggie moved to the refrigerator. Her eyes darted to the space between the refrigerator and the counter where she had seen the gun and prayed that Laurent had not removed it to yet another hiding place or, God forbid, gotten rid of it altogether.

She pulled open the refrigerator door and drew out a large chunk of cheese and some shaved ham.

"Pickles would be good," Richard said from behind her.

Her hands shook as she pulled a jar of gherkins from the refrigerator and set them down on the counter.

The gun was not there.

"I can't slice the cheese with you holding that knife to my neck," Maggie said. She cleared her throat and felt a needle of piercing anger at Laurent.

Where is it now? Where did you put it?

"Try." Richard held the knife to her throat.

"Are you so terrified of me," Maggie said picking up the small knife from the counter, "that you don't think you could disarm me?" She began to saw into the block of Edam.

"I will not be manipulated," Richard said.

Where in hell was that stupid gun? He isn't letting me take a breath, let alone, find a gun, unwrap it, and God knows load it because Laurent surely didn't hide it with bullets in it!

Which means I also have to find the bullets...

Maggie cut three fat and ragged chunks of cheese and then dropped the knife onto the counter.

It was hopeless.

Her hands shook dramatically as she assembled the sandwiches.

"Do you...do you want a plate?" She reached for the cupboard door over her head.

"Of course I want a plate."

She opened the cupboard and removed a small china plate. Before she closed the door, she saw what she did not expect to see and what she wasn't sure was at all important any more.

Pushed back behind the saucers and dishes, she saw a small, unwrapped cartridge of rounds for the Glock.

"Bring it in here," Richard directed, motioning toward the dining room.

Maggie grabbed the plate, her hands shaking badly now, and walked into the dining room.

Richard sat down at the table and motioned for her to do the same.

Without a word, he snatched up the sandwich and took a large bite. He watched her, chewing loudly, his cheeks puffed out by too much food, and then stopped. His eyes looked startled, as if he'd found a small stone in his mouthful.

"Water!" he said through the muffling layers of bread and cheese. Maggie looked at him uncertainly and then was on her feet.

"A glass of water?" she said in her best hostess's voice as she moved quickly to the kitchen.

"And mustard! You stupid cow! You cannot even make a

sandwich. Are you trying to choke me with these dry roof tiles of bread?"

Once in the kitchen, Maggie heard him get up from his chair. She jerked open the cabinet door, grabbed a drinking glass and the bullets in one hand and moved to the sink. Her back to the kitchen door, she shoved the ammunition into the waistband of her skirt and filled the glass with water.

"Get out here, now!" he screamed from the other room.

Her eyes darted around the kitchen for a usable knife, while images formed in her mind of her storming out of the kitchen wielding the bread knife or stabbing herself in an attempt to hide it in her clothes.

She could hear him opening drawers in the dining room, mixed with the sound of candlesticks falling off the buffet and china shattering to pieces. She opened the refrigerator door and grabbed the jar of mustard.

"If I have to come for you," he screamed, "I will cut off something important!"

With the mustard in one hand and the glass of water in the other, Maggie stepped breathlessly into the dining room.

Richard was standing by the buffet. All the drawers were pulled open and he had tied a large linen napkin comically around his neck.

"I'm a messy eater," he said, smiling as he touched the napkin with his fingers. The butcher knife lay on the table beside the half-eaten sandwich.

Maggie remained standing. Her eyes were riveted on the small, partially wrapped package in Richards's hands.

He'd found the Glock.

～

Laurent squinted at the check and grunted.

"*Non, non!*" Jean-Luc said, grabbing without success for the bill.

Laurent sighed.

How long would the man feel in his debt? Were words not enough to forgive the past? What more can he say?

"Jean-Luc," he began, the weariness evident in his voice.

"Hey, you guys! I thought I'd find you here!"

Windsor Van Sant strode up to the café table and tossed his calfskin gloves onto it.

"Grace said you'd probably be here. Glad I caught you. Hey, Jean-Luc, how ya doing?"

Jean-Luc grinned his gap-tooth smile and motioned to a free chair.

Laurent stood and shook hands with Windsor.

"Windsor, it's wonderful you are here," he said. "You were looking for us? All is well? Maggie didn't call you? "

"No, no, nothing like that." Windsor settled into a chair and signaled for the waiter. "Just hadn't seen much of you lately and wanted to make sure I helped you celebrate getting the grapes in."

"*Superbe*, Windsor," Laurent said. They gave their drink orders to the waiter and Laurent tucked the dinner bill under his coaster.

Life was so good tonight.

Laurent felt himself settling in for a long, celebratory evening at the café. He watched Jean-Luc—with his nonexistent English—and Windsor—with his bad French—chat companionably to each other.

I am blessed in so many ways.

~

"Don't you think it's fun to go through people's drawers and see the treasures you find?" Richard said. "I was just looking for *une serviette* and found this! Now that is a good mustard. My favorite, in fact. And did you think to bring a knife to spread it?"

Richard set the handgun down next to his plate and reached for the mustard.

"No knife?" He laughed. "Not as resourceful as I gave you credit for," he said. "I thought all Americans were resourceful."

He unscrewed the lid and dipped two fingers into the mustard.

"But you are not a sly people, are you Americans? Instead, so—what is the word—*up front*, eh?" He used his fingers to spread the mustard onto his sandwich, then wiped them on his napkin at his neck.

Two startling streaks of yellow jumped out from the white cloth at his throat.

"Perhaps to be a little sly might be helpful from time to time, eh?"

He took another large bite of the sandwich and nodded as if to reassure Maggie that this time it was good.

"Might be a useful thing in certain situations that come up." A piece of ham slipped from his thin lips and fell to the tablecloth.

Maggie dragged her attention away from the gun.

"Brigitte wasn't American," she said, setting the water glass down near his plate.

Richard continued to chew but scowled at her.

"But I guess she wasn't very resourceful, either," she said. "For all her being French and everything."

"Shut up," he growled.

Richard finished his sandwich, drained the water glass, then took his napkin and carefully wiped the glass of his fingerprints.

"Can't be too careful," he said.

"I should imagine you could leave your prints all over everywhere," Maggie said, the bullets in her waistband began to pinch. "And the police still wouldn't figure it out. They are so stupid."

Richard frowned.

"They are not that stupid," he said, pushing away from the table. He picked up his knife and the gun. He held it up for her. "Where are the bullets for this?"

"I have no idea. It's Laurent's gun."

"To the couch," he said, motioning her with the knife.

"It's because they're French," Maggie continued. "In America, you couldn't get away with being so sloppy."

Richard's face turned crimson. "What are you saying? That the French police are inferior to the American police?"

Maggie hesitated at the coffee table near the couch. In the mirror over the couch, she briefly caught her reflection and the image jolted her as nothing else had tonight. Her long hair had worked loose from its bun and now hung in a black curtain past her shoulders.

She wore her gray chemise untucked over a slim black skirt. Her pale, heart-shaped face looked shocking beneath the harsh black lines of the vivid X which stretched from cheekbone to brow and from chin to cheek.

She was dressed like a corpse.

Richard walked to the coffee table and dropped the Glock onto it with a loud clatter. He held the knife low at his side, flicking it against his thumb and forefingers and nicking himself as he fidgeted.

Maggie saw that there was nothing left. No hope, no cavalry coming, no chance for her except what she was able to produce against nature. In all likelihood, it wasn't going to be much, probably just enough to lead the police to Richard but not enough to save herself.

She pushed the thought—and the image of her face in the mirror—as far away from her as she could. Bringing Richard down, she thought. Well, that was at least something.

Richard was ranting now.

"The French are superior to the Americans in every way!" he shrieked. "I am simply too clever for the police. That is why..."

"I admit your food is pretty good," Maggie said, forcing herself to move closer to Richard—and to the gun on the coffee table.

Incredibly, now that she was close to him, Maggie picked up a faint fragrance that she recognized as overpoweringly familiar to her.

Her stomach churned with the sudden recognition that Richard was wearing the same scent her own father had worn for years when she was a child.

The scent, at once sweet and clean and male, sent years of images and feelings of safety and love surging through Maggie. She forced her knees not to buckle with the emotional impact.

"Our *food*?!" Richard sputtered.

It occurred to Maggie as she watched the man rage that the climax to this nightmare was likely upon her, and with that thought was the realization that she was angry.

Angry at not being able to see her parents or Laurent again. And angry at not getting the chance to have a baby.

Angry that this piece of killing vermin had the power to unnaturally end her biography, that something so vile and valueless as this piece of walking dementia could subtract her from the population and that there was nothing she or Laurent or anyone could do to prevent it.

And amidst that anger, building with every sickening second, Maggie got a desperate idea. Desperate and futile. But she was barreling her way down a dark and too-slick tunnel to her last moments on earth—she could see that. He had killed before and he was preparing himself to kill again.

Somehow, against all her instincts, Maggie knew that, this time, stalling was not the answer.

"How did a vulgar little toad like you ever get Madeleine?"

"Eh?" Richard blinked as if he hadn't heard her correctly.

"I mean, is there something wrong with her or did she lose a bet?"

The look of astonishment on Richard's face might have been amusing. Any other time.

"You should see how stupid you look right now," she said, doing her best to sneer. "You never answered me about Madeleine. That has got to be the mystery of all time. I mean, I can understand what she saw in *Yves*."

In a burst of flying food particles and a torrent of howling, incomprehensible French, Richard drew back his fist and slammed it into Maggie's taunting face.

She reeled with the blow and fell backward. Richard held the butcher knife high above his head and reached down to pull away the massive tangle of dark hair that shrouded her as she lay slumped atop the coffee table.

His screams continued as he fought with her hair, his knife beginning to slash the air with anticipation.

A noise from the French doors leading to the garden startled him. He dropped the tangle of hair and stepped away from Maggie's body for a moment. He held the knife to his chest as if to shield himself with it and looked through the panes of the doors from where the noise had come. Then, he took a long breath to gather himself and returned to the job.

It was only the little dog.

15

M aggie saw the blow coming and braced herself for it. Her last thought before she blacked out was that it wasn't much of a plan.

Stars erupted in her brain against a background of screaming blackness as she felt the floor give way beneath her. She tried not to give into the faint but it overwhelmed her as she fell, crumpling onto the coffee table between her and Richard.

It felt right to succumb, to allow it to happen, to shut down. She felt herself drift away from the noise and the fear and pain, and the need to do so was great.

To end it all, to just close my eyes, and end it...

Within seconds she was being tugged back to consciousness, the pain roaring through her like a train gathering speed. Fighting a barely recognizable feeling of disappointment to be back among the living, Maggie forced herself to move and to think again.

The rush of fresh pain as Richard pulled violently on her hair, twisting and jerking it, was clearing her head.

She felt the hard, boxy shape of the Glock beneath her on

the table. She could hear Richard screaming at her, although the words were lost to her brain. Her hair cloaked her as she lay with her back to him. Slowly, her fingers—numb and stiff—began to fumble in slow motion at her waistband for the cartridge of rounds.

He jerked her by her hair up off the small table. In terror, she felt for the chamber on the Glock with fingers that felt like baseball mitts.

She forced her mind to focus as she tried to remember the gun with her fingers.

She was fully awake now and could understand his raging.

"You are dead! You are dead!"

He wrapped his fist around a length of her hair.

No! No! Not yet! Please, God.

Her fingers fought to find the chamber opening as she felt herself being lifted, the back of her neck exposed to him. Her fingers plunged into the chamber and with her other hand she tried to position the round for insertion, but it was too late.

As she felt herself being lifted off the table by the roots of her hair, she saw an absurd vision in her mind of her old account executive at the ad agency holding up a pie chart.

Suddenly, the pressure on her hair ceased. Inexplicably, Richard stopped his assault. Somewhere in the back of her mind she heard a small dog's growl and in her mind's eye, she saw Richard step away from her, felt him disengage, and knew immediately—as if she'd been watching it on a movie reel—that the respite was temporary. He hadn't quit for good, just for the briefest of moments.

But, for Maggie, it was enough.

Her hair draping her once more, she slammed the cartridge into its chamber and twisted over onto her back, pointing the gun in front of her.

Not bothering to take the time to push her shroud of hair

from her face, to sit up or to aim beyond Richard's general direction, she fired.

Richard screamed and grabbed his arm. He slashed downward with the knife.

Maggie twisted off the table. The knife sliced into her hair. She scrambled to her feet and held the gun straight out in front of her.

He stood, the knife in his hand, but the other hand was gripping his shoulder which was gushing a small fountain of blood. Rage and pain gathered on his face along with stark surprise.

Maggie's hands were slick with sweat as she held the gun and she longed to remove one from the gun to wipe against her skirt.

She knew she didn't dare.

She locked her elbows in a shooter's stance and took careful aim at Richard's face. He looked like a mad bull about to charge.

"This Glock is loaded with fifteen rounds," she said, wondering where her voice was coming from. "Fourteen in the clip, one in the chamber. There is no safety. Unlike a revolver, a Glock semi-automatic is the perfect lady's choice with the effort to shoot off each round equivalent to the work it takes to press a button on a keyboard. "

Richard looked at her as if she'd lost her mind.

"Put that gun down," he said, his fingers on his good hand flicking the blade of his knife.

"I will. Guns are dangerous. I'm a big believer in gun control."

She moved to the telephone on the side table. Her tongue felt a loose upper tooth and her lip had already swollen to the point she was having trouble speaking. The prospect of balancing a telephone on her shoulder, dialing, dealing with the French operator and keeping Richard—as wily as a mental patient—from sticking his knife in her throat seemed insurmountable.

"Drop the knife," she said.

Richard looked at the phone and as if suddenly seeing her dilemma, smiled.

"I don't think so."

He took a step toward her.

"You shouldn't think I won't shoot you, Richard."

"Madame, you are marked for death. Don't you see? I am not the one who will die tonight. Like Brigitte, like little Pijou... like so many more to come."

She saw his knife hand twitch. She steadied her arms. The Glock felt heavy and she resisted the need to lower it to her side just for a moment.

"You're crazy," she said.

"And you are so American, no? A gun against a knife? I am nearly unarmed! And wounded! You would shoot me?" He laughed and looked almost fondly at Maggie. "I think not. Your very nationality will prevent you from saving yourself tonight."

"A round from a semi-automatic creates a tidy hole upon impact," Maggie recited, forcing herself to take strength in the mantra of her copywriter's facts.

"You cannot do what you need to save yourself. There are no police tonight. There is only one lone *Américaine* who cannot kill a nearly unarmed man." He smiled sadly, shaking his head. "Even to save her life."

He took a step toward her.

"Don't do it, Richard."

She licked her lips and felt her arms begin to violently tremble in her effort to hold the gun aimed at him

"Oh, *Madame*," Richard said softly, his eyes glittering as he moved toward her. "Why is it I just don't believe that?"

Bedard eased the emergency brake on and sat for a moment. He looked up at the house. Surely it made more sense that Marie Pernon or even Grace Van Sant would be the killer's next victim tonight. To come to Maggie's house alone, while sending his men to the other women's homes was to ensure he would be made a laughingstock.

At best, he would not be on hand to apprehend the murderer. At worst, *Mesdames* Pernon and Van Sant would pay the final price for his addleheaded reasoning.

Maggie's car sat alone in the dark gravel driveway. A light glimmered past the curtains of the kitchen.

Quietly, he stepped from his police car and studied the house front. He pulled a cigarette from a pack in his shirt packet and tapped it against his lip, unlighted.

Where was Dernier's car?

It was past midnight and the air had turned cold. He could feel the beginning stirrings of the mistral, the powerful cold wind that sent roof tiles flying all over Provence like so many loose playing cards. If he were lucky, he would be home sleeping in his bed before it struck tonight.

Bedard lit his cigarette and approached the large stone steps of the farmhouse.

He would make his call from inside *Domaine St-Buvard* to hear his men's report. He knew they would be either making an arrest of calling the coroner or perhaps, both. He cursed the instinct that had driven him to come to Maggie instead of accompanying his men.

Hadn't Pijou said her mother Marie was next? The girl had awakened, fully conscious, naming Richard Dupré as her assailant and said he'd bragged that Grace Van Sant and her mother were to be his next victims. And Maggie Dernier.

Bedard tossed his cigarette off the steps into the night. Having heard Maggie's name mentioned—even as third on the list—it was impossible that he could have gone anywhere else.

He raised his hand to knock on the door when the sound of a gunshot exploded from inside the house.

Richard lurched at Maggie, his eyes wide in shock.

She'd shot the gun.

And missed.

With a roar he charged her, slashing the butcher knife downward in a wide arc toward her face. She tried to back away from him.

The knife came down just as she felt the coffee table behind her knees and blocking her from further retreat.

She twisted sharply at the waist and felt the knife as it sliced past her shoulder, cutting away sections of her long hair and skin. She shut her eyes and squeezed the trigger again.

The sound of the blast exploded in her ears, the same sound that only seconds before she'd been too numb and shocked to hear. It seemed to ricochet off the walls of the room and swallow her up with its volume.

Richard buckled with the impact of the shot. A spot of blood formed near his hip and began to spread. The knife, clutched in his hand, hovered above her head as if caught in a freeze frame on a movie screen.

His eyes bulged at her in astonishment, but, instead of falling backwards, he roared at her, spittle flying about his head like sparks. His face was a reddened, puckered picture of frothing insanity. He brought the knife slicing down once more.

She forced herself not to twist away this time but to maintain her balance.

She shot him again.

This time, he gave a terrible groan and stopped, his eyes staring madly at her as if trying to remember who she was. Maggie corrected her aim and held the gun—now feeling like a hundred weight in her quivering arms—high, pointed at his forehead.

Richard licked his lips. They twitched into a spasmodic semblance of a smile. Quietly, he crumpled to her feet, the knife bouncing away from him like a petulant child's discarded toy.

Maggie staggered backwards, tripping once more over the coffee table, as Bedard charged into the living room.

Maggie looked at him and then sank to the coffee table, the gun finally sagging between her legs. He ran to her and stood between her and Richard's body.

"Oh, Roger," she said in a whisper. "Do I have to do everything for you?"

Laurent excused himself and walked to the terrace of *Le Canard*. He needed a moment outside to clear his head from all the drink and the cigarette smoke. He was staring in the direction of *Domaine St-Buvard*. His breath came in long slow visible puffs in the cold air.

He pulled his collar against his neck. The weather had turned. By morning, they would be in their winter coats. He felt another surge of relief that the grapes were in.

Windsor came up behind him.

"She'll be fine, Laurent," he said, clapping a big hand down on Laurent's shoulder. "Without Grace, I mean. She'll be fine."

Laurent looked at his friend and smiled. "Of course."

"I mean it," Windsor said.

The burly American rubbed his cold hands together and blew out a cloud of breath.

"Maggie's tough. Besides, she's got you, man."

Bedard took the gun out of Maggie's hands and bent to examine Dupre. Never taking his eyes from where she sat staring glassy-eyed at Richard, Bedard picked up the telephone and called an ambulance.

He went into the kitchen and returned with a glass of wine and a dishtowel. Wordlessly, he handed the wine to Maggie and tied the dishtowel to Richard's midriff. The man groaned softly on the floor while Bedard worked. When he finished, he knelt facing Maggie.

She put the drained wine glass down on the coffee table. Her hands were shaking.

"How did you know to come?" she asked numbly, her eyes not looking at the body on the floor

"I didn't know. I just came." And this time, when he took her into his arms and held her, she didn't resist.

Maggie wrapped the heavy wool blanket tighter around her shoulders and still she shivered beneath it. She stood on the front steps of the house watching for the jaundiced headlights of Laurent's Renault.

Bedard had called *Le Canard* and told him to come home. Bedard's men were crowded in the tiny kitchen and living room. Two of them were searching her car.

When she saw the ambulance was ready to remove Richard, Maggie went upstairs to change clothes. It was there she discovered her blackened left eye, split lip and bruised cheekbone. She stared into the mirror and saw her hair was matted and chopped in two places, and the blood drying to her silk chemise under a bad cut on her shoulder. She touched the wound gently. It would need stitches.

The black X was vivid against her white face.

Ignoring her wounds, Maggie picked up a tissue, wet it with her tongue, and began to rub at the black lines on her face.

Bedard knocked on her door and came in.

"You're hurt," he said. He lifted her long hair away from the cut. "I'll get the paramedics. "

Maggie tossed down the tissue, her face still marked, and moved past him to the stairs.

"I'll go to the hospital in the morning."

"It could get infected," Bedard said. "I'll take you now in the squad car. "

"Laurent will take me," Maggie said. Her back was to him as she moved downstairs.

Bedard reached out and held her arm. They were hidden in the darkness of the stairwell.

"You blame me for not coming sooner."

"I had no expectation you would come at all."

"I should have been here."

Maggie disengaged her arm from his hand and then gave it a brief squeeze before descending the stairs.

The front door flew open and Laurent entered in a rush of cold air. The heavy door thudded behind him with a loud boom. His hair was wild from the wind, his face was flushed in anticipation and anger and—when he saw Maggie—anguish.

"*Mon Dieu!*" he cried. He took two long strides to where she was coming down the stairs and took her into his arms. He kissed her battered face, his words a medley of English and French.

When he finally drew his face from hers, he looked into her eyes as if to make sure the woman he knew lived still behind those eyes.

"I'm fine, Laurent," Maggie said, wincing from the pain in her shoulder, yet not willing to unravel herself from his arms.

Bedard descended the stairs.

"She saved herself," he said to Laurent. "She didn't need either of us."

Laurent regarded Bedard coming down the stairs from the bedrooms.

The same lackluster sergeant stood in the doorway to the living room. The rest of Bedard's men were piling into the two squad cars out front.

"We'll need a formal statement," Bedard said to Maggie. "Perhaps after your husband has taken you to the hospital?"

Laurent frowned and looked at Maggie. Instantly, he saw the red stain coming through her sweater.

He swore. "We will go now!"

"No, Laurent," Maggie said. "We'll bandage it for tonight, okay? I can't bear the thought of getting in the car. Please."

Laurent touched her hair, her long beautiful hair that now hung in uneven, jagged pieces.

"*Mon Dieu,*" he said again.

He picked her up into his arms and carried her into the living room.

Bedard hesitated, then let himself out.

Several hours later, Maggie woke up next to Laurent. She was stiff and sore. She was thirsty and her lips were cracked but while her shoulder felt achy, it didn't really hurt.

After giving her a brandy and wrapping her in one of her cashmere shawls, Laurent had driven her to the emergency room in Aix where they stitched the laceration in her shoulder and gave her painkillers.

Now, Maggie lay watching her husband sleep, grateful for the drugs and for his gentle insistent love. She listened to the sounds of the mistral outside the house. The shuttered windows rattled loudly as the strong wind dragged across them. She cuddled down under the duvet closer to Laurent.

The noise she heard in the next few seconds made her sit upright.

Petit-Four!

She decided against waking Laurent. Worry can be as

exhausting as pain, she thought, as she slipped out of bed and padded downstairs to the living room.

On her way to the French door where she could see the silhouette of the little dog pawing at the door, Maggie hesitated at the coffee table, which was now carefully repositioned in front of her damask floral couch. She saw the pillows on the couch and the china creamer still on the dining room table.

She touched the coffee table with her fingertips. It seemed to Maggie she could still detect the fragrance of her father's aftershave lingering in the air.

The little dog barked impatiently.

EPILOGUE

Maggie handed Grace the roll of masking tape.

"I can't believe you're doing this yourself," she said.

It was a week after the attack. In a surprising anticlimax, Richard died during the surgery to remove the bullet from his stomach.

It was a surprise because none of his wounds were considered life-threatening. Ironically, Grace suggested that Richard had died not as the result of a would-be victim defending himself but due to sloppy workmanship at the hospital.

The attending surgeon had had too much Schnapps after dinner and before entering the operating room.

Zouzou sat on Maggie's lap, winding the packing twine around her chubby fingers and chewing on the frayed ends.

"The movers would only break my best stuff," Grace said, pushing a lock of golden hair behind her ear. "Besides, it gives me something to do."

"It took me awhile to figure out," Maggie said, combing her fingers through the baby's sparse fringe, "that you really wanted to go home."

Grace looked up from the package she was taping shut.

"Yes, well," she said. "I'm sure you can relate?"

Maggie stood up with the baby and walked across the empty parlor, its walls lined with taped-shut cardboard boxes.

"You know," she said. "That's the funny thing."

Grace stopped working.

"Oh, don't tell me. Don't tell me you like it here now and are ready to settle in because, as my crusty old uncles used to say back in my old Kentucky home, that dog won't hunt."

"You're from New Jersey."

"Same thing. I'm not believing it."

"Things are different now."

"I think I read about this in *Martha Stewart Magazine*," Grace said. "It was an article entitled, 'How to Feel at Home in a Strange Country.' First, shoot some scumbag lowlife, then plant a bed of day lilies near your driveway."

"Very funny."

"I still can't believe you know how to handle a gun. What was all that nonsense about hating them and having a fit when Laurent had one in the house?"

"It's not nonsense. I do hate them."

"But then how?"

"I worked on the Glock account as a freelance copywriter back in Atlanta."

"Excuse me?"

"Well, I mean, handgun makers have to advertise too, right? So I had their account. I wrote the copy. I researched it. The client insisted I become familiar with his product, so I went to the shooting range several times to handle one."

"Was this before or after you wrote the ads for pesticides and cigarettes?"

Maggie tickled little Zouzou.

"Mama's being a be-yotch, isn't she, sweetums? Yes, she is, yes, she is."

"Marie was totally impressed, I have to tell you," Grace said. "Really completed her image of the gutsy American flying to the rescue, six-shooters blazing."

"Before I forget, Laurent said dinner's at exactly eight o'clock but you and Win come early if you can."

"What's he making?"

"I have no idea."

"Not putting it in the cookbook, darling? It'll probably be an extravaganza. You should probably take color pictures. Editors like that sort of thing."

"Speaking of Marie..."

"She told me that René and Pijou are both home. And she's working to put things back together for them. She's extremely grateful to you."

"I wish I could've figured things out before Richard was crouching in the backseat of my car."

"You poor angel. I cannot imagine."

"Madeleine called me."

"From jail, I hope?"

"She didn't know anything that Richard was doing. In fact, *she* thought she'd killed Yves. She'd slipped him a Mickey Finn or something yesterday."

Grace stared at Maggie.

"*Madeleine* tried to kill Yves?"

"She actually thought she *did* kill him when he turned up dead."

"Why did she want to kill Yves?"

"Turns out he hit her too."

Grace grimaced and picked up a delicate china figurine.

"What a lovely man."

"And you were right," Maggie continued, handing Grace a sheet of packing newspaper. "The cosmetic surgery Madeleine had was corrective. Correcting a moment of Yves' pique with her."

"Why did she put up with it for so long?"

"Who knows? Why do any of 'em? In any event, she's moving to Paris. And I've decided to dump the cookbook."

Grace stopped wrapping the figurine.

"What? You're kidding. You're not going to do it?"

"It was never my thing. Not really."

Grace stood up and wiped her hands on a clean cotton cloth on the table.

"All that work."

Maggie gathered her hair behind her head and held it for a moment before releasing it. It spilled in a small page boy style around her neck. She had cut it to shoulder length to even up the jagged evidence of her encounter with Richard's knife.

"I must have been desperate for something to do."

"But now that I'm leaving you're not so desperate?"

Grace took Zouzou from Maggie and the baby laughed.

"I'm going to write a novel," Maggie said.

"A novel."

"A piece of fiction."

"As opposed to a factual recount of the dull happenings near and about the sleepy village of *St-Buvard*, France?"

"A novel."

"The hair looks good, Maggie. Richard did you a favor."

Maggie burst out laughing.

"God, you're perverse, Grace! Anyone ever tell you you're a serious fashion victim? The bastard wasn't trying to give me a trim, you know. Besides, I'm growing it back."

"Of course you are! We wouldn't want to be chic for any length of time, would we? Maybe I can find you one of those Cher wigs for the meantime. I'm sure the iridescent green color wouldn't be a problem for you."

Maggie grinned at her. "I'll never find anyone to take your place, Grace. God knows you're one of a kind."

Grace settled the baby on her hip and draped an arm around Maggie's shoulder.

"I'll miss you desperately, Maggie, back in the real world of drive-through banking and round door knobs. You know I will."

"I'll miss you too, Grace. Truly."

The two friends were silent for a long moment.

"Well, it doesn't have to be forever," Grace said. "One of these days you'll come home to the States."

Maggie nodded and smiled.

But in her heart, she knew for the first time that that probably was not going to happen.

And she was fine with that.

To follow more of Maggie's sleuthing and adventures, order *Murder in Paris, Book 4 of the Maggie Newberry Mysteries!*

RECIPE FOR PAN BAGNAT

A perfect thing to bring to a Provençal picnic! Laurent makes his Pan Bagnat with the following ingredients:

- 4 perfectly red tomatoes, sliced thickly
- 2 green peppers, seeds removed
- 4 spring onions, finely chopped
- 4 artichokes, sliced thin
- ½ lemon
- 12 black Niçoise olives, pitted
- 4 hardboiled eggs, sliced
- 4 good bread rolls
- 1 clove garlic, peeled & cut in half
- 8 anchovy fillets (or canned tuna)
- 8 basil leaves
- red wine vinegar
- olive oil

Cut rolls in half and scoop out some of the interior. Rub with garlic clove. Mix 4 TB olive oil with 1 TB red wine vinegar and soak bread in the dressing.

Lay one half of each bread roll with: tomatoes, peppers, onions, artichokes and olives. Then arrange boiled egg, anchovies and chopped basil leaves on top and season with a drizzle of olive oil. Press the sandwich closed firmly. Leave in fridge for one hour so flavors will blend.

ABOUT THE AUTHOR

USA TODAY Bestselling Author Susan Kiernan-Lewis is the author of *The Maggie Newberry Mysteries*, the post-apocalyptic thriller series *The Irish End Games, The Mia Kazmaroff Mysteries,* and *The Stranded in Provence Mysteries,* and *An American in Paris Mysteries.* If you enjoyed *Murder in the Latin Quarter,* please leave a review saying so on your purchase site.

Visit her website at www.susankiernanlewis.com or follow her at Author Susan Kiernan-Lewis on Facebook.